ACROSS THE GREAT DIVIDE

by SIMON JAMES

SCHOLASTIC BOOK SERVICES
NEW YORK · TORONTO · LONDON · AUCKLAND · SYDNEY · TOKYO

12 11 10 9 8 7 6 5 4 3 2 1   4   9/7 0 1 2 3 4/8

Printed in the U. S. A.   01

To Ysanne, Simon, and Barnaby

Chapter One

As Zach (Zachariah) Coop nudged his horse over the ridge he was feeling on top of the world. The sun was high and warm, the birds were singing, and a cool breeze fanned his heated face. Coop was nearing the high country; the air was crisp and clean.

The sheer beauty of it all was enough to make a man sing from pure joy, and Coop's natural high spirits were heightened considerably by the pocketful of money he had picked up in the last town he'd stopped in. People's enthusiasm for poker, Coop reflected, far outstripped their gambling skill. He slackened the reins, let the roan walk out along the skyline, and belted out a song in his light, high tenor.

"In Dublin's fair city, where the girls are so pretty, That's where I first met sweet Molly Malone..."

The posse moved through tall reeds, the Indian

tracker in front no longer bothering to look for Coop's sign. When a man thinks he's away clear, he gets careless. He might, if he's really confident, even start singing. The Indian reined in for a moment, then set his horse toward a small stream. The trees alongside it would provide good cover. The posse followed, fording quietly, disturbing only the bright pattern of sunlight on the clear, cold water as they reached the slight bank and filed into the shade of the trees. Some of them drew their guns. The Indian pushed his horse on toward the clearing beyond the woods.

"...Cryin' cockles and mussels, alive, alive oh! Alive, alive ooooh, alive, alive ooooh, singin'..."

Still singing, Coop reached down and took a card from the top of his boot, looked at it a moment, then slipped it into the sleeve of his jacket. No, he thought, they'd never learn. People would always want something for nothing. And while human weakness and greed still existed, Zach would be pleased to let them try — and even more pleased to see to it that they failed. He twitched the reins and started down from the crest, surprising a broad-antlered stag that stood stock-still, watching his approach. For a moment they regarded one another curiously, then Coop doffed his hat to the surprised beast.

"Top o' the morning to you, sir. Eh? Well, thank you. That's a fine hat you're wearing yourself."

His roan shied as the stag snorted and crashed away. Coop took up a little slack in the reins, amused that his horse should be nervous about a harmless deer. But when the roan skittered again, prancing slightly crabwise, Coop began to look around, knowing that something besides the stag was spooking his horse.

"Easy, boy. Easy!"

At first he could see nothing. Just the mountains backed by blue sky and cotton-wool clouds, and the lines of fir trees on the lower slopes. Then the posse broke cover, moving out of the trees, kicking their mounts into a gallop as they sighted their quarry. Coop looked at his pursuers in horrified disbelief. "Oh, *no!*" He pulled the roan around hard, clapped his heels to the horse's flanks, and set off at a hard gallop.

The posse spurred after him, except for one man who dropped his reins, steadied his horse, and fired his rifle at the fleeing figure. Coop heard the crack of the gun, then felt a violent tug as his hat was shot from his head. He knew now that the posse was out to get him, dead or alive.

Zach jerked his horse to the left, ducked his head low, and dug in his heels. Then the bullets *really* started flying.

As the slope got steeper, the horses slid and braked on the loose gravel, their riders fighting to keep their balance in the saddle. The distance between Coop and his pursuers had so lessened that the Indian slipped part way off his mount, and hung there, squeezing off a shot. Coop's horse went down from under him as the bullet struck home, and Coop was flung facedown in the dirt.

If he'd had time, Coop might have reflected that this day, which had started out so well, had taken a distinct turn for the worse. Instead, he paused just long enough to suck some air back into his lungs. Then he sprinted madly for cover in the nearby brush.

As the posse began to move in among the young trees, Coop reached the bank of a stream. He slid quietly into the shallow water and began to lope upstream, covering a couple of hundred feet before wading back to the bank. Before he climbed out, Coop carefully lifted a small, flat rock, stepped on the impression it had left in the dirt, then leaped onto the stony ground higher up, letting the rock fall back to cover his footprint. Then he began to climb.

The Indian had tracked many men in his time: some wily, some clumsy with fear, some skilled in the ways of the wild, and he knew that Coop was good. It had taken him three or four precious minutes to work out whether Coop had crossed to the far bank or stuck to the water. Then a tell-tale leaf had come drifting downstream and the uncertainty was gone. The Indian walked against the current with the mounted men behind, moving swiftly but looking rapidly from bank to bank, missing nothing that might reveal Coop's trail. When he saw the small, flat rock near the bank, he didn't pass it up. Beneath the rock, Coop's print was as clear as day. The men of the posse began to push their horses up toward the level ground of the plateau.

Coop knew he had gained a little time. He emerged from the trees at the river's side, brushed himself off, and halted for a second to get his bearings. That was when he saw the wagon.

It was in a small clearing just beyond the trees. One wheel was shattered, and the wagon itself was tipped at an angle. But what interested Coop was the fact that tethered to it were two horses and a foal, all lazily cropping grass and looking to Coop like the answer to his unspoken prayer. He moved toward the wagon, slowly at first; then, seeing no sign of life nearby, he broke into a run. The nearer of the two horses, a chestnut, raised his head as Coop came up to him, then started grazing again as knowing hands moved reassuringly over him, patting his neck and testing the lithe muscles.

"Hold it right there, Mister!"

Coop's back stiffened. For a fleeting moment he wondered how the posse could have come up on him that quickly, that silently. Then his panicking brain registered the voice properly and he turned around in amazement.

The girl was a little under five feet. She wore her blond hair in twin braids and was, perhaps, thirteen years old. The other thing Coop noticed was that she was pointing a man-sized rifle right at his belt buckle. And she looked as if she knew how to handle it. Coop raised his hands. For a moment nothing happened, no one moved. Then a foxy black and brown mongrel snaked out from under the wagon and began a furious barking.

Coop looked down in surprise and backed off a little. When he recovered, it was to find not one kid but two regarding him with stern faces. The girl, still with an unwavering bead on Coop's midriff, had been joined by a boy of about nine who sized the intruder up for a brief minute, then came to a quick decision.

"Get him, Charity," the boy yelled at the dog. "Bite him!"

"Hey, get outta there!" Coop backed off again, and dropped his hands to ward off the dog who had taken a firm grip on his boot and was worrying it to the accompaniment of a series of bloodcurdling growls. The girl swung the rifle to keep the be-leaguered Coop covered, shouting, "Get your hands up!"

The boy was altogether more positive. "Shoot him in the leg!" he urged.

"Now hold on, boy! I was just admirin' your horse."

The whole situation seemed more than a little crazy to Coop but with that rifle aimed so unerr-ingly at him, he figured a friendly approach was the right one. He smiled a smile that had been known to charm the birds down from the trees. "Is your pa around? I'm in the business of buyin' horses."

The boy stood in the full light of that dazzling smile and, without taking his eyes from Coop's face, said, "Don't trust him."

The girl obviously had no intention of doing that. She took a step forward and the muzzle of the gun came up. "He's not for sale," she said. "Now back away from that horse."

This wasn't just a crazy situation, thought Coop, it was fast becoming a desperate one. That posse couldn't be far behind, and right now he would have given all but his dealing hand for a good horse. He advanced on the girl slowly, talking as he moved.

"I can see you have a special feeling for this animal, Missy. But these here are extenuating circumstances...." He broke off as the girl brought the rifle to bear on a spot right between his eyes.

"Hold it right there," she rapped.

Coop stopped dead and held up a hand in mock surrender, but he kept talking. "I'm willing to pay you ten times what the animal's worth." He paused and put some emphasis on his next words. "Five hundred dollars."

"Five hundred dollars!" echoed the boy, some interest in his voice.

Coop heard him, but continued to talk to the girl. "That's a lotta money, Missy."

By this time the boy had thought it over. "More'n you got," he sneered.

Coop looked hopefully at the girl.

"That horse is the only way outta this territory..." she said. Coop waited. "...and we're not plannin' on sellin'."

Coop knew that he had wasted more than enough time. "That's your mind?" he asked.

"That's my mind," the girl replied firmly.

"Then I'll be on my way." He turned and began to walk away across the clearing, covering only a few feet before the girl called out to him.

"Where you headed?"

"Over those mountains." Coop pointed up toward the vast, snow-covered peaks of the Rockies — the high country he'd been making for until the day had changed from one of peace and easy traveling to a time of flight and near death and kids with guns.

"Oregon?" asked the girl.

"That's right." Coop wasn't sure, but he began to feel that maybe — just maybe — his luck was changing. The kids looked at each other thoughtfully. Then the boy said firmly, "Don't do it."

The girl shook her head. "We have to," she replied softly. Then, raising her voice, said, "Hey, Mister! Maybe we can come to some other arrangements between us."

Coop brightened. "What's that?"

"If you'd be willing to let us ride along with you, we'd be willing to loan you a horse till we reach Oregon."

Coop moved back to where the kids stood beside the wagon. Suddenly they both looked small, despite the gun, and lost.

"There's just the two of you?" he asked.

Holly nodded. "That's right. You can ride double, cantcha?"

Coop smiled to himself. At that moment, he'd have happily shared a horse with the devil himself. "Yes, ma'am," he agreed, "I can ride double."

The Indian waded out of the stream with the posse strung out behind him. Starting at the bank and leading up toward the ridge were clear signs of Coop's passage: signs that not even the best backwoodsman could have hidden from a real tracker. He had drawn his pistol now, sensing that Coop couldn't be too far away; the trail was faint, but it was unmistakable — and it was fresh. The riders followed him up the rise.

Coop lifted a saddle and bridle out of the wagon and hefted it toward one of the horses. Holly watched him, still not quite trusting the stranger, but knowing that without him the chance that she and Jason would make it across the high mountains to Oregon was desperately poor. With a professional eye, she watched Coop saddling the horse. Then she asked, "Think we can make it to Oregon before the end of the month? We have urgent business there."

"I don't see why not, if we get going right away." Coop sensed some real concern behind the question. "What's your business?"

"We've inherited some land there. But if we're not in Fort Williamson by May thirty-first, it goes to the next of kin. And he's the most stingy, undeserving, miserly nothing in the world."

Jason had been listening to this, and added his comment: "Besides, he's ugly!"

Coop tightened the cinch on the horse and turned

back to glance at Holly. "Gets your hackles up, huh?"

She laughed and nodded. "Whenever I think about him."

Then her laugh faded and she busied herself with repacking some belongings that had come loose when the wagon wheel broke.

The land in Oregon was important to Holly and Jason, just as it had been important to their grandpa. Well, Grandpa was dead now, and Holly knew that if only she and Jason could get there in time, they could claim the land, and make something of it as their grandpa had wished. Maybe it was crazy — two kids out on their own trying to make a near-impossible journey to lay claim to a patch of land they'd never seen. But they were determined. It was all they had now, all they hoped for. And it was rightfully theirs — if only they could get to Oregon on time.

Coop slipped the bridle on the horse. Then without turning to face her, he asked Holly, "How come you're out here on your own like this?"

"A fella hired on to help us after Grandpa died. He up and stranded us after the wagon busted."

Jason came up alongside Coop and held the horse's rein. He added: "He took more than forty dollars of our savings too."

Coop smiled down at the boy. "You just can't

trust anybody these days," he agreed.

Holly climbed down from the wagon where she'd been packing a sack of their belongings. Already she was beginning to feel better about Coop's arrival. "It was an act of Providence that you showed up when you did."

Almost as she spoke, she saw some movement: a flicker at the corner of her eye. Men and horses were coming over the skyline, moving quite slowly at first, but then prodding their horses into a gallop. Coop had seen them a second or so before she did. It took him just one more second to get into the saddle and slam his heels into the horse's flanks. Jason leaped out of the way as Coop took off, low over the horse's neck and riding all out.

At first, Holly and Jason were too shocked to move. Then Jason yelled, "Hey!" and Holly screamed, "Come back!" as Coop and their horse hammered across the meadow. Jason's next move was to grab the rifle and cock it. Holly snatched it from him. At that moment she was just as mad as Jason, but she knew she was the better shot.

"Gimme that," she shrieked, and drew a bead on Coop's rapidly fleeing figure. Jason didn't mind who fired the bullet — as long as it found its mark.

"Shoot him," he bellowed. "Don't just stand there — *shoot him*."

Holly's finger tensed on the trigger. Then the

first rider in the posse crossed her line of fire and the chance was gone. But if Holly couldn't get a shot off, the men of the posse certainly could. Bullets whined through the air as the horses drummed past the wagon and the outraged kids. In the midst of the dust and noise, Holly's voice could just be heard. "Hey, Mister," she bellowed, "don't shoot. That's our horse he's riding."

One of the tail-enders reined in, turned his horse and looked down at Holly and Jason in mild astonishment. In all the confusion, no one had really noticed them.

"What are you kids doing out here?"

"We're on our way to Oregon," Holly yelled up at him.

The man pulled his horse around in order to get a clearer view of the two children. Oregon? Clearly they didn't know the country, the risks involved, didn't understand just what they were getting into. He figured that their parents must be somewhere around — a whole family bound for disaster on the high peaks yonder.

"Oh, now, you tell your pa to turn back. It'll snow for another month up there. You're crazy!" Then he brought his horse's head around again, to follow the rest of the posse. By this time, Coop was not much more than a dot on the far horizon.

"Who is that man?" shouted Holly.

The rider checked his horse momentarily. "A card trickster," he replied. "Robbed the whole town..." Then he slapped his horse's neck with the loose rein and joined the chase.

Holly threw the gun down to the ground in disgust, as she and Jason turned to face each other. "I knowed it!" Her face was puckered with anger. "I knowed it all along!" Then her fury left her and she stood like someone defeated, saying nothing. Finally, she turned wearily back to the task at hand.

"Jason," she sighed, "get the other horse."

Jason wore the expression of someone who had been ignored, but finally vindicated. "You should have listened to me," he said self-righteously.

It was enough to make Holly good and mad again. What with the hired hand taking off with some of their money and Coop's thieving — it was all too much.

"That scoundrel," she exploded. "That greasy, smiling vagabond. No one's gonna steal from the Smith family and get away with it again!"

Trailing dust, the posse rode out of sight. Jason stood and watched them go, feeling, despite his justified anger of a moment ago, vaguely sorry for the man they chased. He hadn't, after all, seemed a really bad case. He thought about Coop — on the receiving end of all those bullets.

"Poor feller," he muttered.

Holly's head snapped up. "I'd like to skin him alive, that two-faced jackal!" She swung up on to their remaining horse and reached out to help Jason mount.

"Well," he said, as he pulled himself up behind her, "if you'd listened to me none of this woulda happened." Somehow, though, the conviction had gone out of his voice.

"He buffaloed me," retorted Holly. "He pulled me in with that sweet-mouthing nature of his."

There was nothing for it, of course, but to leave the wagon now. They could manage a few provisions. And they would take the foal they'd been towing along since they'd started out with their grandpa. The foal, and Charity. The two animals ran alongside as Holly kicked the horse into a trot.

The tiny procession rode away from the broken wagon toward the high, white, fearsome peaks of the Rockies, Holly still grumbling venomously. "Hope he drops dead from anthrax poisoning," she spat. Then, trying to think of something infinitely worse: "Hope he falls on his head, and loses his mind."

As it happened, Coop was beginning to feel that he *had* lost his mind. There was bad luck, he thought fleetingly, and then there was *bad* luck. For a while it had seemed that he was getting clear — the kids, the horses, his clever maneuvering in the stream to throw the posse off the scent. Then, suddenly, he was on the run again, ducking bullets and pretty sure of a lynching if they caught up with him.

He needed just one piece of fortune — an ace in the hole, a pat hand, the Lady's touch on his shoulder. And as the thought flashed across his mind, the luck came. He topped a crest, with the posse in full sight, and saw below him a herd of wild horses, disturbed by the approaching riders and already begining to mill nervously. With a whoop of joy, Coop rode for the center of the herd, approaching at a hard gallop and stirring them up as he had hoped. As he rode among them, the posse came abreast of the hill, the Indian in the lead, pointing in Coop's direction.

They gave chase as Coop raced straight into the herd. The wild horses wheeled, scattered slightly as they panicked, then with one accord took the pace of Coop's horse and began to gallop bunched, so that he was all but invisible among them. By the time Coop had spotted some cover, his pursuers were no more than halfway down the rise; and he was out of sight to them for just long enough to take his chance. As the furiously running herd came abreast of a thick stand of trees, he reined in savagely, turned his horse in among the leafy branches, held his breath, and waited. As the last of the wild herd thundered past, effectively obliterating his tracks, all Coop could hear was the violent banging of his own heart.

The posse came past looking neither to left nor right, spurring toward the disappearing herd. Coop waited for a while — long enough to know that no one was coming back. Then his shoulders slumped with relief and he allowed himself a smile.

Just like I always say, he thought, *when you're lucky, you're lucky.* He moved out of the trees and set off at a fast clip away from the direction taken by the posse — but not directly away. Before him, almost near enough to touch, it seemed, were the snow-capped mountains. Coop paused and looked up briefly to where the blindingly white peaks cut into the hard, bright blue; then he shook the reins and the horse began to stretch again.

He'd been riding for some time before he came to the stream. He'd heard it, though, before he'd seen it; had known it was there, too, by the way his tired horse had begun to pull, wanting to break into a trot. Coop was as thirsty as the horse. Frantic riding, dust, and fear had left his tongue almost cleaving to the roof of his mouth.

He jumped down and the horse waded past him into the stream. Coop lay flat on his stomach and, putting his face in the stream, sucked up the cold, clear water, gulping again and again, feeling it cool and restore him. Then, gathering up his horse's reins, he half-turned to go on his way when a voice made him freeze. It was a voice he'd heard before — but this time it was good and mad.

"Just one move..."

Holly's aim was as steady as ever. The gun didn't waver; it was pointed at Coop's midriff, just as before. And Coop had little doubt that there was a shell in the chamber.

"...just one little twitch..."

Coop had no intention of twitching. In fact he was trying not to blink or breathe. Only his thoughts were moving—in the direction of desperation and defeat. How many times can a man's luck change in a day?

"...and I'll blow your scoundrel head off!"

Jason was as direct as ever. "Just shoot him!"

Coop thought quickly. "You'll have every Indian in the territory down on us," he warned.

Holly sneered. "I'd sooner face a thousand Blackfoot than deal another second with you... you thievin' trickster! Now" — she gestured slightly with the gun — "put your hands on your head."

Jason moved in, carefully, and led the horse to the bank.

"Look," Coop tried a reasonable tone. "I was planning on coming back just as soon as we got rid of that po—" He realized his mistake. "...those bushwackers."

"Bushwackers?" Holly laughed. "Decent people, you mean. People you just recently robbed. You're an unending liar, Mister."

"Just go ahead and *shoot* him!" Jason urged.

Coop stood there, his hands on his head, and waited. For what seemed like half a lifetime, Holly continued to squint down the barrel of the rifle. Then, addressing her remark to Jason, she said, "Start movin' out."

Coop watched the horse being led away and made one last frantic appeal to Holly.

"My whole life's fallin' in ruins."

"It's your own doing!"

"Look, there's no denying it, Missy. Circumstances have forced me to behave less than truthful...but it's circumstances and not an evil nature that's to blame."

Holly was having none of it. "Hogwash!"

"I don't know why you just don't *shoot* him!" yelled Jason.

"Hey, boy...." It seemed to Coop that Jason was altogether too free with his advice. He took half a step. Holly snapped the gun up.

"Get down, or I'll shoot your leg out from you right now!"

Bending awkwardly at the knees, his hands still

clasped on top of his head, Coop sank down. As best he could, he looked up at Holly.

"Well, what're you plannin' to do?" he asked.

"Put as much distance as I can between us and your low, evil cunning." She began to move back to where Jason was holding the horses. Coop rose unsteadily to his feet.

"Missy," he said, "you can't make it alone." He took a faltering step toward her.

Without a flicker of hesitation, Holly squeezed off a shot at almost point-blank range and just a couple of inches away from Coop's left foot.

"Stay back, Mister," she snapped.

"Are you crazy?" Coop staggered back, regarding the girl in horrified amazement. If he'd ever wondered whether Holly would actually fire the gun, he was in no doubt now.

Holly stood as steady as a rock. "You better get down," she snapped. "Right now!"

"You almost killed me!" Coop dropped to the ground once more, still watching her anxiously.

"You're lucky I wasn't aiming at your head." She turned away, surer now that Coop would stay put. "Let's get on, Jason."

The children mounted, Holly still looking back and keeping the rifle pointed at him, as they nudged their horses into a walk. Jason looked across at his sister.

"What're we gonna do now?"

"Keep on going," Holly answered. "Turning back now would be like giving up the whole future."

There had been a little uncertainty in Jason's voice; a touch of fear. The country around them looked frighteningly wild and the mountains ahead were impossibly tall. He trusted his sister; he always had. Since the wagon had broken and the hired hand had run out on them, there had been little time to take stock of their problems. Now the excitement was over — the excitement of the posse and of the horse thief, presently kneeling by the stream, watching them go. Coop was a rogue, Jason was sure of that. Shooting was probably too good for him. Even so, he didn't quite seem like a villain.... And Jason had his own private fears about what dangers might lie between the two of them and that patch of land in Oregon.

All he said to Holly was, "Hope you know the way."

Looking toward the looming peaks of the Rockies, Holly gave her answer. "Straight ahead."

Quite alone in that wilderness, atop horses too big for them, without knowledge of what lay in store or any real certainty of how they would survive, the kids took up their journey again.

If Holly worried that maybe — just maybe — the task ahead of them was too great, she made quite sure that her fear wasn't obvious to her brother; and if Jason was, well, worried that Holly might be worried, he gave no sign.

As they moved away from the stream, Charity and the foal trotted after them, the dog scurrying after the foal, nipping its heels, making the animal skitter and buck. The country around them was wooded: lush green grass muffled the sound of the horses' hooves. Holly knew that there would, at least, be plentiful game — if they could hunt it. But always in view was the snowline; and above that few things — animal or human — could survive for long.

Chapter Two

Zach Coop watched the children's departure with mixed feelings — mixed, but all bad! Humiliation, annoyance, fury.... To be jumped by a couple of kids that way! It was shaming! Now here he stood, in the middle of nowhere, lacking a horse, provisions, a weapon to hunt with — not even a blanket for the cold nights.

The small procession of kids, foal, and dog was two-thirds of the way across a meadow and heading into the far treeline. Charity was still harassing the leggy foal, barking and making it run. Coop paused a moment, then shrugged. There was only one course open to him — he knew that. With a little sigh, he started after them.

The children had been riding for some time before Holly deigned to look back over her shoulder to see how well Coop was keeping up. She had known for quite a while that he'd been following them. At first she thought he might give up, or at least stop to rest and fall back out of sight. But there he was, plodding along in their wake and not seeming to tire.

Coop saw the glance backward and smiled inwardly. He'd known that she had known he was there. It was a game of pretense, with a lot of pride mixed in. She wouldn't acknowledge him; he wouldn't attract their attention. That was to the good as Coop figured it. After all, they could have spurred on at any time, leaving him with the tiresome job of tracking them and trying to make up lost ground. He was still mad, but by this time most of his anger was directed at his own foolishness. He strode out, his jacket over his arm, chewing on a piece of grass and grumbling at himself.

"Look at you, Zach! No horse, no supplies, not even a rifle. Hah! Can't even talk two kids into a deal. You're losin' your touch, boy. Ohhh...if Poppa could see you now!"

Coop's natural good humor was creeping back. Squaring his shoulders and lengthening his stride, he kept the children in view as they crossed a patch of rocky ground and began to ford a small stream. A few yards from them a young moose stepped hesitantly into the water, then gingerly lifted its hind legs one by one and shook them, as if becoming accustomed to the new element.

At the sight of something fresh to chase, Charity took off barking wildly, pursuing her startled victim into deeper water. As she crossed the stream, Holly watched the chase for a short time, confident that, although Charity loved to run and bark and play the hunter, she would never hurt anything unless it threatened the safety of herself or her brother.

She turned again to look back at Coop. He was closer now; but although she felt some annoyance at the fact, Holly felt no fear. Oh, she knew that Coop was a gambler, a liar, a horse-thief.... How much money he must have tricked out of honest folk in his time! She was sure that he was the last person she and Jason wanted on the difficult journey ahead. Like Jason, however, Holly felt that Zach was not a vicious man, though there was no doubt about it — he'd steal their mounts, guns, food, anything he could lay a thieving hand on!

With the children some fifty yards downstream of him, Coop knelt down to drink again. Brilliant chips of reflected sunlight spilled over his fingers like liquid diamonds. Then he stood up, smiling to himself. His good humor was returning.

For most folk, good fortune was a nice surprise: not looked-for, but more than welcome, of course, when it came along. Coop knew that luck had to be courted, expected, even helped along a little. Part of being lucky was being receptive to luck. You had to look for Lady Luck wherever you went, then get her attention and set out to woo her. Pretty soon, she'd start to recognize you, and if you didn't ask too much, she'd be there, likely as not, when you needed her most.

Well, maybe Zach had been asking a lot of her lately. And he'd thought, at first, that she'd run out on him, what with the posse coming so close and then the kids leaving him stranded. There was another way of looking at things, though. The posse *hadn't* caught up with him; he *had* come on the kids — and their horse — at just the right time. Now here he was, still alive, on a warm day in beautiful scenery, apparently out of danger and happily trailing a couple of kids who would surely wake up, in the end, to the fact that they needed him more than he needed them. That was another thing about Zachariah Coop: he was an optimist.

The children rode out of sight, down into a little glen fringed with spruce, and as Coop topped the small rise behind them, his feeling of well-being took over completely. Snatching up a long stick he waited a second, till Holly glanced back as he knew she would, then began prancing to and fro, lunging with the stick, his left arm held high behind him in a comic parody of a swordsman.

Silhouetted on the skyline, he thrust and parried, retreated and advanced, defeating scores of adversaries with brilliant swordplay. The children looked on, not quite sure how to take all this. Then, overcome at last by sheer weight of numbers, Coop suffered a mortal rapier cut, staggered dramatically this way and that and finally keeled over and rolled down the slope. He lay still for a short while, enjoying the scent of the springy turf, before peeking to see whether the kids were still watching. They were — riding on slowly but gazing back with what seemed, to Coop, a new, almost friendly curiosity. Or was he simply imagining that? It was too far for him to read the expressions on the children's faces accurately.

He got up, dusted off his pants and began to follow, glancing toward them again as he did so. That was when he caught the flicker of movement, just beyond them and off to the right. The kids saw it too; and then they saw what it was.

The Indians were stock-still, sitting their mounts like statues just outside the cover of the treeline. Their eyes tracked the kids' progress across the meadow.

Holly knew that the Indians wouldn't have been

seen unless they'd wanted to be seen, but she wasn't at all sure whether this was good or bad. *Bad*, she decided at last. *After all, they can't imagine that me 'n' Jason would give them much trouble.* She could see at least six of them, and knew there could be more still concealed by the trees. Jason shortened his horse's rein, guessing that at any minute they'd have to make a run for it. Holly signaled to him to keep his horse at a walk. Any display of fear, she figured, would set them off. The kids continued across the field. Both kept their eyes firmly fixed on the motionless Indians.

"They just keep on starin'." Jason tried to suppress the fear in his voice.

"Just carry on like nothing's happening," Holly instructed.

Almost as she spoke, the Indians started across the meadow at an easy canter.

"Here they come," yelled Jason.

Before the Indians made their move, Coop had quickened his stride, trying to make up ground without appearing to hurry. He knew they'd have spotted him too. And he'd certainly been watching them since they first appeared on the fringe of the trees, attempting to read the signs.

They weren't wearing paint — that was good, but it didn't necessarily mean there was no danger. Nor were they, now that they'd started to move in, galloping flat-out toward the children; but then again, the chances that they would be outrun by the kids weren't exactly high. He hadn't heard of any Indian trouble recently, not that he could recall. But he hadn't heard that there *weren't* any hostiles nearby. Coop wasn't sure. With Indians, you were never sure.

Jason and Holly reined in and waited, their mouths dry, their hearts booming in their chests.

"What if they start shooting?" Jason asked, almost resigned to the fact that they would.

Grimly, Holly drew the rifle from its saddle holster. Her palms were wet against the smooth wood of the stock, but her mouth was set in a determined line. "We stand and fight!" she replied, gripping the gun but keeping it turned away from the Indians and flat across her pommel. Then they were surrounded, looking anxiously this way and that as the Indians kept a tight circle. Charity growled, trotting around the group of horses.

The Indians rode alongside for a few strides and, for a second or so, did nothing. Then a young brave leaned over and grabbed Holly's rein close to the horse's mouth, speaking as he did so.

"What?" Holly's question had more to do with the brave's intentions than with whatever it was he might have said to her. He turned the horse and despite her tugs on the rein, Holly found herself helpless, unable to bring her horse around, or see what was happening to Jason.

"What are you doing?" she snapped, her indignation rising, despite the panic she felt. "Let go of my horse!"

It was as if she hadn't spoken. Ignoring her protests, the brave leaned over again and snatched the rifle.

"Gimme that back!" She made a lunge for it, but missed. As the Indian continued to lead Holly's horse, her indignation swelled into real anger. If she'd stopped to think, she'd have realized that since she couldn't understand a word her captor spoke, it was just as likely that he couldn't make sense of her. Nonetheless, she half-turned in the saddle, facing him, and snapped, "My name is Holly Smith and I come from a good family."

The Indian remained expressionless.

"We're going to Oregon!" Holly continued, her voice rising. "I demand you let go of my horse this instant!"

At that moment, she heard another Indian behind her say something and she remembered her brother. Her anger mixed with a fierce protectiveness. She became aware that these were not just strange, threatening, half-naked primitives — they were warriors and had, or so she'd heard, scant regard for human life; especially, she imagined, for the life of a captive.

"Jason!" She yelled to him, wanting some reassurance, and tried to turn in the saddle to see what was going on. The Indian at her horse's head continued to tow her along.

"You'll live to regret this day, you — you heathen savages!" Her voice became tinged with panic. "I'll have General Miles Carson himself *personally* revenge this outrage!"

At this point — and just as Holly was beginning to feel that things were getting severely out of hand — Coop arrived on the scene. Clearly, the Indians had seen him coming. Clearly, there had to be some sort of confrontation. What wasn't so clear — especially to Coop — was what the outcome of that confrontation might be. The leading horses, those ridden by Holly and the young Indian, came up to where Coop stood. Zach planted his feet firmly, looked up at the Indian with what he hoped was an unflinching stare, and waited.

The Indian looked down at the figure barring his way and said something to Coop in that same guttural tongue that had jarred so on Holly's ear. *Savages' talk*, she thought. Then she was amazed to hear Coop answer in the same language. She peered at Coop; and it seemed to her that his face was a lot less worried than it had been some sec-

31

onds before. Coop and the Indian continued their conversation, Holly looking from one to the other with growing frustration.

"What's he saying?" she demanded.

Without looking at her Coop replied, "He wants to know why you're making me walk behind." Then he continued his parley, using extravagant gestures to emphasize what he was telling the Indians. As he went on, one or two of them started to smile; then there was an odd chuckle. Then, as the Indians looked from Coop to Holly in astonishment, the laughter grew to roars of delight.

Holly and Jason were so confused and uncertain about the story that Coop was giving that they forgot to be relieved. *If they're laughing at me...* Holly thought sternly. *What story's he telling them?* She put the thought into words. "What'd you tell him?"

We're not clear yet, Missy — he tried to signal it with his eyes, but continued to smile broadly, feeding the Indians' humor. Still keeping his eyes on the braves, he replied, "I was drinking and you're punishing me."

This was too much for Holly. "Don't listen to a word he says," she yelled at the Indians. "He'll tell you anything to save his mangy hide!" If anything, Holly's anger made them laugh harder. The Indian let go her rein and tossed her captured gun over to Coop; then he said something, speaking through his laughter, and wheeled about, gesturing to the other braves to follow.

They were a long way off before Coop took his eyes off them. Finally, he stepped up to Holly's horse — still smiling; and now his smile was genuine. Not unreasonably, he was expecting a word or two of thanks. Holly's face was like granite. "You insulted me, didn't you?" It wasn't really a question. Zach decided to lay the blame on the Indian. "He said, 'All men must stick together or women'll rule the world.' "

"That's right, Mister!" The derringer seemed to come from nowhere, leaping into Holly's hand as if by magic. With her arm extended, she held it a couple of feet from Zach's head. "Now hand back that rifle, butt first."

Coop groaned in disbelief. "Oh, we're not gonna go through all that again, are we?" Looking up past the wicked little gun to Holly's determined expression, he could see that, yes, they *were* going to; and, as before, he was going to come out the loser. Still, he held on to the rifle with as much resolution as he could muster.

"I'm not foolin'." The girl's finger flexed slightly on the trigger. Coop believed her. He was a poker player and a good one — he knew when not to call a bluff. Holding the rifle by the barrel he held it out to her.

"Slowly!" Holly cautioned. She leaned over

slightly and took the rifle from him. Then she ordered, "Back away!"

Coop did as he was told, feeling understandably hurt by the children's ingratitude. Feeling, too, that if Holly chose to, she'd make a great card player. Right now, hers was the only game in town. Maybe, he thought, it was time for a little more sweet reason.

"You can't make it over those mountains alone," he insisted. "Can't you understand that?"

Holly ignored him, pushing the rifle back into its scabbard, but keeping the derringer aimed firmly at his head. Coop's tone became exasperated.

"You need me as much as I need you!"

Holly shook her head. "You don't need us, Mister," she replied, almost sadly. "You just need our horses. Come on, Jason." She picked up her reins and the pair of them moved off, Holly looking straight ahead, Jason looking back at Coop's unmoving figure.

Zach could see the apprehension in the boy's eyes. The incident with the Indians had ended well — but Jason had clearly been shaken by it. He was, after all, a very small boy in a very big, and often very dangerous, country. His eyes met Coop's; and in them was a mixture of determination and worry — a look of stubbornness and childish uncertainty that brought a lump to Zach's throat.

He watched as the kids once again turned their horses' heads toward the vast, natural barrier of the Rockies and his expression grew serious. Though Jason was well out of earshot now, Coop muttered, "Good luck, boy." There was no bitterness in his voice — just concern. Luck wasn't something he often wished to other people. There wasn't enough to go around. But those kids, reflected Zachariah Coop, were going to need more than their share.

Later that same day the children found a place to camp, in a wooded area beside a fast-flowing stream. They knew from experience that it was better to make camp while there was still light, before the sun got too low in the sky, to be sure the campsite had wood for a fire, water, and maybe food, within easy reach, and good cover.

Holly set Jason to cooking a fish they had caught. The boy had built a good fire and as Holly completed her chores, the delicious smell of frying fish rose in the air.

With great care, she was tying a thin rope around the tops of four sticks that marked out their site, making a small barrier between their encampment and the surrounding wilderness. Inside the rope square, the horses cropped grass contentedly. Holly would finish off by fixing a small bell to one of the taut ropes: a warning system, should anything — or anyone — attempt to enter their camp while they slept.

She tied the bell and sat back, anticipating the mouth-watering dinner Jason was preparing.

"Boy, that cookin' smells good!"

Jason looked up as she moved toward the fire. Reflectively, he tilted the fry-pan to move the fish around.

"Think he's gonna catch up with us?" he asked after a moment's silence.

It was a question that had been on their minds for some time. Holly picked up a bedroll and began to lay it out.

"He'll be here," she replied, deciding, as she spoke, that she knew it to be true. "He's too mean to die on the way."

"Well, what're you going to do?"

"Depends on what *he* does."

Jason watched his sister spreading the bedroll on the ground; then, noticing that the fire was getting a little low, he began to fan the flames with his hat. He pondered Holly's reply, then asked, "What d'you think he *will* do?"

Holly seemed pretty sure about that. "Steal the horses," she said, "and leave us to die out here like the lyin' tyrant he is."

"He wouldn't do that."

Holly turned on him indignantly. "He already did it, didn't he?"

"He said he'd bring back the horse," Jason retorted.

"Now you're falling for his tricks!"

She spread out a second bedroll, while Jason looked glum, knowing that she'd won the argument. She was probably right, Jason reflected sadly. A villain never really changed his ways.

Not more than fifty feet away, Coop was watching the children's camp from cover. Downwind, more out of habit than real caution, he was getting the full benefit of Jason's frying fish. Like Holly, he had to admit that it did smell good. He crouched there, observing that they certainly seemed to know what they were doing. They were tough kids, he thought, and brave; likeable, too, despite what they'd put him through. He knew, though, that it would take a lot more than bravery to see them across the Divide and safely into Oregon.

A tiny breeze wafted the scent of the fish directly under Coop's nostrils, teasing him, making him realize just how hungry he was. What with the day's exercise and excitement, together with the clear, clean mountain air, he felt he could eat a riverful of fish. Squaring his shoulders, and testing his most winning smile, he decided to take another crack at wearing down the kids' defenses.

He looked about him till he discovered a piece of wood about the length and general size of a walking-cane. Then he tied his scarf around one end of it and stood up, dusting himself off. As he began to advance on the camp, he heard Charity give a couple of growls, followed by a short, sharp bark of warning.

Holly and Jason looked up and saw Coop at once. Holly gestured to the dog. "Lie, Charity!" she ordered, not looking down at the dog but keeping her eyes firmly fixed on Coop as he advanced. Charity continued to emit little growls and whimpers, her body tense with inaction.

"I think he's repentant," offered Jason.

"He's beyond that," Holly scoffed. "Not even the angel Gabriel could save his soul." Despite herself, she smiled as she made this last remark. Coop really did look rather woebegone out there on foot with his flag of truce. He kept coming — slowly but surely.

"Ahoy!" he yelled. "Anybody home?" The children remained silent. Undaunted, Coop continued with his speech. "I was just passin' through and I saw your fire..."

The kids sat with their blankets covering their legs, still not answering or moving — except that Holly's hand was sliding almost imperceptibly along her blanket on Coop's blind side. "...so I thought I'd invite myself to dinner."

The last word was just out of his mouth when Holly's first shot clipped the side of the stick he was carrying. He staggered back in shocked surprise. The second shot kicked up a small plume of water at his feet. Without more ado, Coop abandoned his flag of truce and dropped down behind a tree.

Holly's eyes fixed on the place where she had seen Coop fall out of sight. She ejected a spent cartridge from the rifle and pumped a new one into the breech. Then she yelled, "Don't push it any further, or we'll do what we have to!"

Coop lay still and kept silent. Then he rolled over, extracted a flask from his pocket, and took a long pull on it.

The children waited for a reply. Jason looked nervously at his sister.

"I think you got 'im!"

"I couldn't have." Holly's assertion was touched with the merest uncertainty. *Who knows*, she thought, *a lucky shot* ... She waited a little longer, still hoping for an answering shout. Nothing. "Hey, Mister!" she called; and then again, *"Hey! Mister!"*

Coop began to realize that he might have an advantage here. He waited expectantly. Then Holly said, "Are you hurt?" Coop moaned in what he hoped was a realistic manner. The kids looked at each other, real concern, now, in Jason's eyes.

"You got 'im." The boy's voice trembled.

"I *couldn't* have," Holly insisted, more in an attempt to convince herself. Coop released another, louder moan and then another, pulling on the flask between times and smiling to himself. Perhaps he just overdid things a little, though, because Holly, hearing the agonized groans coming from behind Coop's tree, smiled to herself. Addressing Jason, but raising her voice so that Coop should hear plainly, she said, "I think we got 'im, Jason. Now what we gonna do?" Then, in a much lower voice, she added, "Keep on talking. He's foolin'."

She moved silently in a wide curve that would keep her out of Coop's line of vision and bring her up behind his position.

For his part, Jason wasn't sure; but he knew he'd better play along for Holly's sake. Speaking loudly, he said, "Maybe we should put him out of his misery. Cut off his head..."

"Let the ants eat him." Holly suggested, still moving up on Coop.

"Maybe we'll have to bury him in a hole nine feet deep," Jason went on.

Coop wasn't really listening. He could hear what seemed to be concern in the children's voices, however, and he continued to oblige with what seemed to him completely convincing moans of agony.

"Or maybe we should dump him in the river!" Jason was warming to his subject now. "Tie a rock on his foot and let him sink to the bottom!"

Coop moaned again, and took another sip from the flask, just as Holly came into view above him. He didn't see her. She watched him for a moment, pleased that her guess had been correct. Then, as he tilted the flask for another drink, she loosed off a shot that came almost painfully close. Coop leaped in panic and slid a full twenty feet down the slope. He slipped the flask back in his pocket, stumbled in getting to his feet, and looked up at Holly in horror and indignation. Holly raised the gun again.

"Don't play games, Mister," she warned.

Coop looked at her over his shoulder — a withering glance, to let her know what he thought of her self-righteous attitude. Holly remained unwithered. She watched, gun at the ready, until he moved away down the slope; and not until he had backed off a way into the bordering trees, did she turn and make her way back to the camp.

The fish would be eaten by now. That was the one thing on Coop's mind. They'd have eaten the fish. He imagined the hot, succulent, white flesh and his mouth watered. It would be just bones by this time... bones picked clean by the two hungry children. Coop's stomach rumbled loudly.

Sighing, he reached out to a nearby bush, plucked a few berries, and with a mournful expression on his face, began to eat them. Grimacing slightly, he picked some more, but as he did so, a small rock rustled and bounced through the light undergrowth past his hand. Coop looked up toward the place the rock had come from. Then something altogether bigger and softer than the rock tumbled down toward him: a rolled up blanket, which Coop caught. As the blanket unfolded, a large hunk of bread fell out of it. Coop looked up again and saw Jason regarding him. Wordlessly, the boy turned away, returning as quickly and as silently as he had come.

Be grateful for small mercies, Zach, thought Coop to himself. He spread the blanket over his legs and began to attack the bread.

Night had come quite suddenly — silken, black, and silent. First there had been the deep, vibrant blue of twilight, with sudden harsh birdcalls in the stillness and the hard silhouettes of trees. That had seemed to last no time at all. Then, as if with a fast rush of blackness, night had descended on the high country.

There were a few big stars strung out in the sky, but no moon; and the sounds were spookier now. The only reassuring noise was the river's soft rumble, or the occasional ripple and splash as it lapped its banks. A coyote yipped and bayed — a chilling, mournful sound that seemed to be very close at first, but then faded into the dark.

The children lay in their blankets, eyes closed, but not sleeping. The fire burned brightly, fueled by the supply of logs Jason had gathered to see them through the night. Fire, they knew, would keep predators away. It was also a reassurance just to have a little light — to be able to watch the glow of the flames flickering around their encampment.

Jason looked straight up at the stars glimmering in the inky blackness, then glanced over to where Holly lay beside him.

"You awake?"

"Yes." Holly opened her eyes.

Jason paused. Then he allowed himself to say what was on his mind.

"Think we're gonna make it?"

There was a pause before Holly replied. "Of course we are," she said, injecting into her voice as much certainty as she could muster. "That's a silly question."

A bird screamed nearby, making the horses stir uneasily. Both children looked anxiously toward the place where the sound had come from, then relaxed again. Jason was calmed by Holly's positive tone; though knowing his sister as he did, he wasn't completely convinced that she felt quite as brave as she appeared. He pulled his blanket up to his chin. "I wish Gramps were with us right now," he said.

Holly looked up at the dark heavens. "He's with us," she whispered. "He'll always be with us." She felt hot tears creeping into her eyes, but thinking of Jason and his fears she stifled her sudden need to cry. They lay with their thoughts for a while, Jason finally shaking off the mood of melancholy. It was his turn to be strong.

He looked again at Holly. "Tell me about Oregon," he demanded.

"Well." Holly considered a moment. "It's the richest land in the world. Every mountain's filled with gold. And the rivers are so heavy with fish that at certain times of the year you can walk across on their backs."

Jason chuckled, as Holly's inventions grew wilder.

"There's so many ducks and geese flying around," she went on, "that the well-dressed ladies always carry umbrellas to protect their gowns."

This was too much for Jason. "You're pulling my leg!" he protested.

"No, I'm not. It's true," said Holly.

They laughed together, then fell silent until

Jason said, "I just can't wait till we get there."

Holly heard the strain behind his words. "Neither can I, Jason." She watched the fire as it sent up a tiny ribbon of sparks into the darkness. "Neither can I."

Chapter Three

Holly awoke to a fine, bright, crisp morning. The tinkling of the bell had made her open her eyes in alarm. Then she saw a fawn, about the size of Charity, investigating the camp. She sat up and nudged Jason awake so that he should see the tiny intruder.

Aware of the movement, the fawn skittered nervously. Then as Jason came awake, so did Charity who had been curled up in the boy's blankets, providing warmth and companionship. Dog and fawn saw each other in the same instant and the chase was on, the fawn sprinting around the camp with Charity yelping delightedly and attempting to cut off its retreat. The children smiled as they watched the fun, knowing that Charity meant no harm to the small creature. Soon, though, they began to break camp. That morning they had a real obstacle to overcome. Ahead of them, barring their way, was a fast-flowing river that had to be forded, and it was deep and strong.

Coop was still asleep. He was not an early riser, and since he had lain down hungry, he was going to get up hungry, and he was in no hurry to do so. His empty stomach was Coop's first thought as he opened his eyes. His second thought was that something alarming had brought him awake. The notion was there in his mind, though he couldn't fix on what it was. He looked around dozily for a bit, trying to work out what was wrong. Then he heard again the sound that had awakened him: the sound of Holly's voice yelling her brother's name. It came from the riverbank.

Coop sat up, and as he did so Holly's voice came to him again through the trees.

"Jason!"

Coop quickly rolled out of his blanket and with his boots in his hand made for the river.

"Don't get too far downstream! She doesn't like the water!" There was more concern in Holly's voice now. Coop emerged from the trees at the riverside and took in the scene.

On the far bank, Holly was sitting on her horse

with Charity draped over the saddle and the foal alongside. She had forded the river first, trying to find the safest route for her brother to follow. At this moment he was in midstream; and he was in trouble.

The river was wide and it was cold and it was fast; fed by streams that came down from the snow-line, it flowed quickly, often treacherously, between steep banks. It was difficult enough for a grown man to control a strong and frightened horse and at the same time beat the strong current in order to make the far bank. For a small boy, it was nigh impossible.

Jason had been riding ever since his legs were long enough to enable him to sit in a saddle. But right now, he simply hadn't the strength to hold things together. With each passing second he was being pushed downstream; and though he fought to turn the horse's head toward the bank and push against the weight of water, he was fast losing the battle.

Charity sprang down from the saddle as Holly dismounted and ran to the lip of the near bank. She felt fear, like a fist of cold, take hold of her, but she refused to panic. Cupping her hands around her mouth, she shrieked instructions at her brother.

"You're getting too far downstream!"

"Hold on to the horse!" Coop yelled advice, too,

as he made for the water, watching the boy's unequal struggle with both the current and his scared horse.

With the river's roar filling his ears, it was unlikely that Jason could hear much. Even so, Holly continued to yell. "There's a big hole right there, Jason; be careful!"

Almost before the words had left her lips, she saw Jason's horse founder, rolling the boy violently sideways into the river. Holly's eyes widened in anguish, but still she kept control. "Hold on to the horse, Jason!" she yelled. It was the only chance: Coop saw that too and called out to the boy, amplifying Holly's instruction.

"Jason, hang on to the saddle!" Then Coop broke into a fast run, making for a place on the bank opposite to where Jason struggled to maintain his grip on the pommel.

Coop hit the water at the run, a long low dive that took him well clear of the bank, and began to swim toward Jason. The river was cold — numbing — and as he swam, Coop could feel the firm tug of the current towing him in a long diagonal.

Jason's hands were losing their strength, his grip on the saddle weakening. He allowed himself only one moment of despair, yelling, "Holly!" and "Help me!" Then, realizing that fear was the one thing most likely to cause his downfall, he gritted his teeth and renewed his fight against the battering of the river.

He was just about sure that he'd lost — could just begin to feel his numb fingers refusing to obey him and slipping from the wet leather — when Coop reached him and began to haul him ashore. On the bank, Holly gasped and closed her eyes in relief. She may even have offered up a short prayer of thanks.

When she opened them again, Coop was helping Jason through the shallows. They both looked very wet and very, very cold. A whole series of conflicting emotions suddenly beset Holly. She felt relieved, of course; she also felt angry; and, most upsetting of all, she felt grateful. To hide her confusion she set about collecting wood for a fire.

Wrapped in blankets, Coop and Jason crouched before the fire as Holly wrung out their sodden clothing and set it to dry. There was something unspoken between Holly and Jason. A question that hadn't been asked, but was understood; an answer that hadn't been given, but showed in Holly's stern expression. Coop looked from one to the other, amused, understanding what was going on.

Finally, Holly broke the silence, unable to bear any longer the hopeful, inquiring looks her brother was giving her.

"We still can't let him ride with us, Jason."

"Why not?"

Holly added more wood to the fire and glanced across to where Coop was sitting, in full earshot, but acting as if he couldn't hear.

"'Cause there's no telling when his low nature will take over again." The children looked at each other: two pairs of eyes, both with defiance and determination in them. They didn't often argue, but when they did there was a whole lot of stubbornness on both sides.

To Jason, things were quite clear. They were beholden. Coop had saved his life. And, in any case, that surely proved that the man wasn't as bad as Holly had been insisting. When he spoke again, Jason's jaw tightened and his expression was obstinate.

"Well, I'm not goin' on without him!"

It was as if Holly hadn't heard. She held Jason's shirt out to dry better before the fire. He tried again.

"We gotta trust him."

Coop had been gathering wood, giving the kids a chance to argue things out — pretending to busy himself, but staying close enough to eavesdrop. It was time, he figured, to add what he could to Jason's defense of him. He moved toward the fire carrying an armful of sticks; and as he passed Jason he asked, "How you doin', boy? Warmin' up?"

Holly turned from the fire. "We thank you for what you did, Mister," she said coolly.

Coop laughed. "Just tryin' to be neighborly."

She kept the ice in her voice. "It was a brave thing and we appreciate it." Then she turned back, leaving Jason and Coop to exchange a speculative glance. Jason summoned his courage, looked at the stiff set of his sister's back, opened and closed his mouth once, then said decisively:

"I'll let you ride double with me from here on in…"

Coop smiled at him.

"…if you want to, Mister."

Coop nodded, still smiling. "Thank you, Jason. It's very considerate of you."

Holly said nothing. She knew when she was beaten.

They had been riding for a couple of hours, getting into really steep country and beginning to feel the chill in the wind. Jason wrapped his arms around Coop's waist and hung on as their horse took a particularly tricky incline. When the ground leveled out a little, he continued his conversation with Coop.

"How come you learned to speak Indian?" He was recalling that the incident at the river mightn't be the first time Coop had saved their skins. Holly, riding just behind them and still exhibiting a stony, disapproving face to the world, pretended to take no notice of this new friendliness between Coop and her brother.

"Well," Coop replied, "my mother was the daughter of a Cheyenne chief."

Jason was impressed. "Really?"

"Yes." The boy couldn't see Coop's amusement.

"What was she like?"

"Don't really remember," Coop told him. "She died two years before I was born." And he looked over his shoulder, grinning at the boy.

"You're foolin' me." They laughed together, Jason reflecting that Coop told almost as good a story as his sister. At that moment, Holly came past them, riding easily, her face still stiff with disapproval. Coop tried some charm. "Beautiful country, Missy."

Indeed, it was beautiful country. The sky was a high, fragile blue, the air crisp and tangy, the pines a bright, brittle green against the majesty of the snow peaks. If Holly noticed it, she didn't react. Unspeaking, she trotted on, looking the other way and radiating injured pride. Coop regarded her back, but addressed himself to Jason. "Is she always like this?"

"Only when she doesn't like you," said Jason helpfully.

Coop sighed. "They're all the same," he said, in a worldly-wise fashion. He added: "You watch this. I'll cheer her up," and he pushed his horse on to catch up with Holly, riding alongside her in silence for a while until he said, "Have you ever seen a picture of the Czar's daughter?"

He looked for a reaction but got none, so he pressed on. "Well, I was just telling Jason here that there's a remarkable resemblance between the two of you." Still nothing, but he continued in hope. "She's considered to be one of the great beauties of Europe, you know that, don't you?"

Holly shook her head — but whether she was indicating that she hadn't known about the wondrous beauty of the Czar's daughter and her uncanny resemblance to that royal personage, or merely expressing weary resignation at Coop's attempt to soften her up was anyone's guess. Coop had a nasty feeling that it was the latter, since she then trotted her horse up ahead of them, offering not one word. *Failed again*, he thought. To Jason, he said, "That's okay — just gonna take a little time."

Jason, though, knew the extent of his sister's determination. He'd seen it operating before; it was something to be reckoned with.

"I wouldn't bet on it," he said to Coop's back.

He'd certainly picked the wrong thing to say

there. "I'd be willing to," replied Coop, taking the challenge.

"How much?" Jason knew when he was on to a sure thing.

"How much you got?"

"Three dollars."

Coop reached his hand around to shake with the boy. "You got yourself a deal!"

The subject of this wager began to walk her horse along a crest above a deep, rich valley with thick clumps of pines on its slopes and on the valley floor. Jason and Coop followed her, looking from side to side and luxuriating in the sense of ease these beautiful foothills gave, when all at once Jason pointed and said, "Down there!"

Coop followed the line of the boy's outstretched arm and saw the deer at once. They must have been downwind of it, he knew, since it was grazing unconcernedly. The slightest sound, the hint of a movement, would disturb it, though, and put the beast to flight; and Coop knew just how important it was that they should get their provisions when the chance presented itself. He was also reminded of just how hungry he was.

"You see it?" Jason asked.

"Good eye, Jason." Coop slid smoothly out of the saddle, motioning to Holly who had also dismounted and had taken the rifle from its scabbard.

She walked quickly toward Coop and Jason, who were kneeling and looking down at the still motionless deer. Coop half-turned to her and held out a hand.

"Give me the rifle."

"I will not!" Holly was horrified at the idea.

"There's a deer down there; come on!" muttered Coop impatiently.

But Holly was having none of it. The rifle was power and she had no intention of passing that power over to a man she still didn't trust.

"If there's any shooting to be done," she insisted, "it'll be done by me."

Coop noticed that the deer was wandering, still grazing, toward a stand of trees.

"All right, but hurry up," he urged.

Holly sighted down the barrel, drawing a bead on the deer, holding her breath as her finger tightened on the trigger and preparing to breathe out evenly, as she had been taught, at the moment when she squeezed off the shot. Her technique was perfect; the animal was squarely in the sights; it was an easy shot. There was just one thing wrong. Holly couldn't bring herself to shoot. She closed her sighting eye for a moment, opened it again, tried to take a grip on herself, failed utterly, and lowered the rifle in defeat. "I can't do it," she whimpered.

With one swift motion Coop took the gun from

her, and that movement was enough to start the deer running, making for the trees with terrific speed. He rose to his feet, tracking the animal with the rifle, and got off one shot while the deer was still ten or so feet short of cover. It stumbled, then dropped: a dead weight.

Jason whooped. "You got 'im!"

Coop smiled and pointedly handed the rifle back to Holly. Then he started down the hill. "Let's go, Jason," he called, and the boy trotted after him.

It was a matter of a couple of minutes before Coop reached the deer, with Jason close behind. *Meat for a week*, thought Coop. Then he heard the sound that no one — especially a man on foot in wild country — wants to hear; but it was a sound that no one could mistake.

He checked, and in a brief second he saw the source of the sound. What he'd heard was a low, booming roar — like a distant rockfall or the beginning of an earth tremor. What he saw was a huge bear; and it was coming straight for him out of some brush not more than fifty feet away.

Obviously, the bear had been stalking the deer, too. And, as far as he was concerned, this was his deer. Now something — someone — was threatening to steal it. That enraged the bear. He was only too eager to enter the fray.

Coop, however, wasn't so ready to do battle for

his dinner. Not with this opponent. The bear reared up, roared, and dropped on to all fours again to run. In that same moment, Coop took to his heels, yelling at Jason as he did so, "Get outta here! Go!"

Jason didn't need telling twice. He sprinted back up the slope toward Holly, while Coop raced off down the valley, leaping rocks and crashing through the brush with the bear in full pursuit.

Up on the hill, Holly frantically worked the lever of the rifle to bring a shell into the chamber, but there was no time to get off a shot. Jason had reached her now, and together they watched Coop running out of sight, the bear seeming to gain on him with every stride. Holly took Jason's arm and started down the slope. "Stay close to me," she told him. "Come on!" Charity and the colt could tell there was danger around from the children's actions. The colt ran and checked and ran back again, while Charity whimpered and went belly-down behind a log. The kids raced after Coop and the bear, managing to keep them in sight as they crashed through low bushes. They could plainly hear the bear's growls and Coop's frenzied passage.

Coop was moving over the rough ground at a speed born of fear. And he knew he couldn't keep it up for long. His legs were beginning to tire, his breath was sawing at his lungs, and his chest hurt as if he'd cracked a rib. He could only manage to stay ahead for a few moments longer.

As he came out of the trees on to the bank of a river, his pursuer was no more than ten feet behind. Just ahead of him was a tall, slender pine, its lower branches some eight feet off the ground. Coop could hear the thudding of the bear's paws at his back. He ascended like a bird, found a purchase on the smooth bole of the pine as if by magic, and scrambled into the lower branches just as the bear reached the tree and reared up to grab him.

The massive paw missed Coop's boot heels by the merest fraction of an inch; that spurred him on up the narrow trunk and into the higher branches. The tree swayed a little and Coop grabbed at a branch to steady himself. Then, his breath coming in great, rasping gulps, he peered down toward the ground. The bear was standing upright, its forepaws high up on the tree's trunk. It paused momentarily, as if to think. Then it gave a shove. The tree swayed again.

When she and Jason arrived on the scene, Holly took in what was happening: Coop treed and with no way of escape that she could see. With trembling hands she raised the rifle and got off a shot at the bear. Either her hands were shaking, or she was breathing heavily from her run — whatever the reason, her shot was wild. The bullet clipped the tree an inch or so below Coop's feet. *Dear Lord*, thought Coop in panic, *if the bear don't get me, she will!* As if to emphasize the point, the bear roared and shoved again at the tree. Coop reasoned that he had enough trouble up in the swaying tree, without running the risk of being shot out of it.

"Don't shoot!" he yelled at Holly. "Just get outta here! Go on!"

He scrambled a few branches higher, wondering where the bear had learned its apparently faultless method for shaking poker players out of trees. *Just my luck*, he thought, *not only is it good and mad and very, very dangerous, but it can also think!*

The bear shoved some more, pushing rhythmically with its massive forepaws, skillfully using the tree's own momentum to rock it to and fro. There was gigantic power in those enormous shoulders. Slowly but surely, the tree began to yaw over toward the river, bringing Coop way out over the water. With a final heave, the bear toppled the tree. Roots tore out of the earth, ripping as the tall pine heeled over completely, dropping ever faster toward the river.

"Oooooooooooooooooooooh!" With a great yell, Coop loosed his hold on the branches, jumping clear of the tree as it crashed into the river. For a while there was no sign of him; then he surfaced in a violent *whoosh!* of spray and began to swim as fast as he could downstream, looking back, as best he could, to see what the bear would do. Maybe, after all, this *was* a bear that could think, for it seemed to ponder the situation before setting off along the bank, keeping pace with Coop and watching him.

Coop clove the water, swimming powerfully with lunging strokes and a strength born of desperation. As the water grew shallower, the riverbank became less steep. He guessed it was just a matter of time before the bear took to the water.

Almost as the thought crossed his mind, he heard a splash and saw the vast, brown bulk coming cross-stream toward him. He looked around, anxiously. Just ahead was a beaver dam and Coop used his remaining strength to reach it, swim underneath — evicting at the same time its angry occupant — and crouch there shivering. He could hear the bear wading up. The cover of mud and loose sticks, he thought, looked heartbreakingly fragile. Between the dam's latticework he could see slivers of sky and white wisps of cloud. Then everything was blotted out by the overwhelmingly large figure of the bear looming above him.

The children had watched the bear bring the tree down and had seen Coop's dramatic fall into the river. After that, they had lost track of him, though they'd followed the bear's progress along the riverbank, taking care all the time to stay behind the beast so as not to attract its attention. They soon realized where Coop's hiding place was, though, when they emerged from the riverside trees to find the bear in midstream, sniffing at the shaky structure of the beaver dam. They watched, their hearts in their mouths, not knowing what to do or how to help.

If it was true that the bear could smell Coop, it was also true that Coop could smell the bear. It was a scent that brought terror: pungent and inescapable in the dim recesses of the dam.

He tried to keep his teeth from chattering and hunkered down beneath the canopy of branches, praying for invisibility but knowing full well that by this time the animal had worked out where his prey was holed up. There was a sloshing sound as the animal circled the dam, looking for a weak point. Then it reared up, impatient and angry, and swiped at the tangle of sticks with a paw. The whole structure shook. Coop cringed back, unable to do anything but wait and hope.

The bear lunged again, sending branches scattering in all directions. Then it attacked the dam in a frenzy of anger, dismantling great chunks. Coop felt real terror now. He covered his head with his arms as debris rained down on him, mud and sticks clattering into the water and more and more daylight showing through the great, ragged gaps in the dam. As it had done with the tree, the bear leaned on the dam and shoved it back and forth, loosening and shaking it. His roars seemed deafening now. Holly and Jason watched helplessly; and for a second, Jason made as if to go toward the river — an instinctive move; more a gesture than a positive attempt to do anything to aid Coop.

"Wait here!" Holly ordered. She, too, was dismayed at the utter impossibility of doing anything to prevent what now seemed to be Coop's certain death.

More of the dam caved in. Sticks and mud splashed inside the flimsy bowl where Coop crouched as the bear smashed and mauled to get at his enemy. Then, as if the miracle Coop had been praying for had been suddenly granted, the pounding stopped. The bear dropped on to all fours again, waited a moment as if making up its mind, and then began to wade purposefully away.

Maybe it had got tired. Or bored. Or perhaps it had thought of urgent business elsewhere. But as animals will, and for no good reason, the great beast decided to abandon the effort. Leaving the nearly demolished dam, it splashed steadily away through the shallows. Coop took what seemed his first breath in five minutes. *When you're lucky*, he thought, *you're lucky*. Nonetheless, he stayed put until he was sure that it was safe to emerge.

He peered up through the debris and realized that the bear was out of sight. He also realized for the first time that he was cold, and soaked through, and weak with a mixture of fear and relief. Holly and Jason, still anxious, ran part way into the river.

"Are you there, Mister Coop?" Holly called.

"Has he gone?" a voice answered.

"No." The irony was heavy in her voice. "He's standing right here beside me."

Coop surfaced through the wreckage of the dam and regarded her sternly.

"What happened to you?" he demanded angrily.

"What do you mean, 'What happened to me?'" Holly asked indignantly.

Coop looked at her in astonishment. Had they been on the bank, just watching, while the bear had pawed and clouted at the dam?

"Why didn't you shoot him?" he snapped.

"Well, you said for me to get outta there," she reminded him.

Coop couldn't believe it. "That was when I was up in the tree! Didn't you see me fall out?" He regarded the children with scorn, then started to wade toward the bank, muttering to himself angrily.

"I've never *had* such a string of luck. People

tryin' to kill me! Horse shot out from under me! Kids turning against me! Grizzlies...!" Something else struck him as the cold water splashed around his thighs. "...and I ain't eaten in three days!" He glared at the children. "Now, you know what that'll do? That'll drive a man crazy!"

Neither child spoke, both taken aback briefly by Coop's sudden rush of fury. Then Jason said meekly, "But...he didn't get the deer."

"He didn't?" Coop's thunderous expression lightened.

"Nope."

Coop considered this information. "Well," he said brightly, "things are beginning to look up!"

Jason took a strip of meat, still skewered to a sharpened twig, from where it was hanging above the fire. Despite the fact that it was burningly hot, he bit into it hungrily and chewed with relish. The rich, dark meat tasted wonderful.

It had taken the three of them some time to get back to where Coop had dropped the deer; and in any case they were traveling cautiously — just in case the grizzly was still around. Then came the task of skinning and butchering the animal. Finally, though, they had been able to get down to the very serious business of eating. By this time, night had fallen and the fire provided some warmth and security, as well as serving to roast their venison.

Coop squatted before the flames, adding fresh strips of meat to a thin pole suspended over the fire by two forked sticks. Jason chewed and swallowed, repeated the process, and then broke the silence with one of those sudden, out-of-the-blue questions. Jason was a boy who thought a good deal before he spoke; and when he did speak, his remarks could come as something of a surprise.

"Do you have a religion, Mr. Coop?"

Zach was taken aback, but he answered straightforwardly. "I was raised a Christian."

Jason pondered this reply, then broached the subject he was really leading up to. "Are you really a trickster?"

Coop saw where the conversation was leading and smiled to himself. It was a fair enough question, though, and he tried to give the boy an honest and sensible answer. "Oh, I think most people are, Jason, at a certain level. But remember this" — he leaned forward and took some meat himself — "you can't trick a man unless he's aiming to trick you."

"How come?" Jason wanted to know.

"Well," continued Coop, "because people in general like the idea of gettin' something for nothing — and the trickster affords them that opportunity."

Holly, her mouth full, was listening to this exchange with mounting annoyance. *No* amount of explaining was likely to cause her to feel that Coop's tricky activities were justified.

"But like all good things," Coop went on, "it must come to an end."

"And they lose!" Jason concluded.

Coop laughed, and added more meat to the cooking pole. "There's a tendency for that to happen, yes," he agreed.

Jason was becoming intrigued. "How do you do it?" he asked.

Coop laughed again. "That's the trick!"

"Could you show me?"

This was too much for Holly. "There'll be no gambling here," she snapped.

"Why not?" Jason demanded. He was eager to see what Coop could do. If it was enough to get you chased half across the county by a posse, then it ought to be something pretty spectacular.

Holly was adamant. "Because I say so!" she retorted, glaring at her brother. She'd already been defeated in one argument — about whether Coop should ride with them at all — and she wasn't ready to give way this time. Jason, on the other hand, was remembering his recent victory and feeling that maybe the time had come for him to stop giving in to his sister's authority all the time. He returned the glare and said, "I don't need you to tell me everything." Then with great assertiveness, he added, "I already got hairs growing on my chin!"

That was more than enough to fire Holly's anger. "I don't care if you're as hairy as a monkey," she shot back at him. "It's when you're smart that counts — and I don't see that happening yet."

Jason opened his mouth to continue the battle, then saw the light of determination in his sister's eye and decided to knuckle under. There were times, he knew, when it was best not to cross Holly. This was another occasion when he was going to come second best. Coop, who had been observing the little conflict, smiled and decided to offer the boy some consolatory advice.

"Jason, she's right."

Holly looked up, surprised to be receiving support from this unlikely quarter.

"Tricking and gambling are just like the devil and whiskey," Coop continued. "They'll sneak up on a man and afflict him before he knows what's happened." He nodded in a sad, wise manner — making just a little too much of it for Holly's trust to be maintained. Then he sighed and continued: "It's a terrible sad thing, a gambler. He's one of the downtrodden people of this earth."

Jason regarded Coop seriously, looking for the signs of dejection, defeat, and a lifetime of being ill-used. "You don't look too bad," he remarked, smiling up at Coop.

Zach persisted with the act. "Ah, looks can be deceivin'. Believe me, beneath these smiling Irish eyes" — he paused for effect, looking first at one child, then the other — "is a heart of stone."

"You mean the Blarney Stone!" chipped in Holly, who was smiling too, despite herself. And suddenly they were all grinning, feeling for the first time a real companionship with one another.

Even Holly had to admit that since his early, scandalous escapades Coop had behaved well... even nobly on one occasion. For one thing, he *hadn't* run off with the horses; he'd probably saved Jason's life, and behind his flowery talk she felt a real warmth and humor. *What's more*, she thought as she looked at him crouching by the glow of the campfire, *he's really quite handsome.*

Could it be that things really were going to be all right after all? Although she'd never let Jason suspect it, she'd been worried — badly worried — from that moment when the wagon broke and the hired hand lit out with part of their savings in his pocket. There could be no turning back, she'd always known that; but she'd never been too certain of just how they were to keep going forward.

We have a chance now, Holly reflected, *we have a real chance.* Some loose brands toppled in the fire, sending out a billow of sparks and a rush of sudden warmth; it reminded her of how chill the nights were becoming. Invisible, but always a formidable presence in Holly's mind, the Rockies towered in the blackness: great monoliths of stone and snow with the cold winds pouring off their peaks. She shuddered and moved a little closer to the fire.

Chapter Four

As usual, Holly was awake early, nudging her brother and rolling immediately out of her blankets to greet the day. Charity and the foal were already active, playing and eager to be off. The kids took a hasty breakfast and then started to break camp, looking over from time to time to where Coop still lay, sleeping soundly with his blanket drawn up around his ears.

Finally, the horses were saddled, the children's few belongings stowed, and the embers of the fire scattered and doused. Holly regarded Coop's inert form with amazement. Just how could anyone sleep so long — and so soundly?

"Check your cinch," she ordered Jason. "I'll go wake him up." She walked the few paces to where

Coop was sleeping and stood over him. "Mr. Coop?"

In the dim recesses of his dream, Coop was conscious of something disturbing him — someone calling his name, or that's what it sounded like. He twitched, tried to ignore it, failed, and then snorted and spluttered a little as he came to the surface of sleep: like a man who has been swimming underwater comes up for air. To Holly, none of this seemed very promising. She raised her voice. "Mr. *Coop*!"

A head came out from under the blankets and regarded her blearily. The eyes were open but with a look in them that suggested his brain was still asleep.

"Are you sick?" Holly asked him.

Coop stared at her blankly. "Huh?" Then her question registered. "No, why?"

"I never seen anybody sleep so late unless they was."

"Well," Coop rubbed his eyes and tried to locate the sun still below the tree line. "What time is it?"

"It's light enough," Holly told him, adding, "It's *late* enough!" She started off across the camp to where Jason was holding the horses. Coop raised himself on one elbow and looked around at the now empty camp, at the dead fire, at the horses saddled and ready for traveling. Holly's pace didn't falter.

"Where you goin'?" Coop yelled after her.

Holly replied without bothering to look back. "We're leaving!"

Coop stumbled out of his blankets, cold and only half-awake, and getting angrier by the second. "Wait a minute," he called, "I haven't had my coffee yet. I can't wake up without my coffee."

"You should have thought of that earlier," Holly retorted.

Coop couldn't believe his ears. "I was *sleeping* earlier!" he shrieked, desperately trying to find his boots, while tucking his shirt-tail into his pants at the same time. Holly was unmoved by his pleas and excuses. She was willing to admit that he wasn't all bad; and he could be an entertaining talker — like last night. But not even his good looks could excuse him for wasting precious time. She reached the horses and turned to watch Coop's antics as he hopped in a tight circle, trying to get his left boot on without falling down.

"You've got ten seconds or we're leaving without you," she threatened.

"Ten seconds!" Coop exploded. "It takes longer 'n' ten seconds to stand up!" The left boot was on; now he teetered in the opposite direction, wrestling with the right one.

"Five..." Holly was counting.

Coop gave up the fight with the boot, threw his blanket over his shoulder and, carrying the remaining piece of footwear in one hand, hobbled unevenly over to the horses, saying, "I've never met a more cold-blooded, unfeeling —" his unshod foot came down on a sharp rock and he yelped — "man-hater in all my life! I swear, you enjoy making people suffer!"

Unrepentant, Holly swung up into the saddle. "We have urgent business to attend to," she remarked rather haughtily, "and I have no intention of missing it because of your laziness."

With a grunt, Coop forced his right foot into its boot. "That's right," he sneered. "Uncle Stingy, huh?"

"You may think it's funny," replied Holly, hurt by Coop's lack of understanding, "but our whole future's at stake and we're not losin' control of it to some stingy, miserly nothing!"

Coop hauled himself into the saddle, pulling Jason up behind him. He realized how important it was to the kids to get to Oregon on time; it had to be — they'd already risked a lot just to get this far.

"Huh, well," he said gruffly. "I can certainly understand that, Missy." Then he added pointedly, "No one likes living under a tyrant. Right, Jason?" Having delivered that blow, he clicked his tongue at the horse and set off out of camp, with Holly glaring furiously at him.

They rode in silence for short time. Then Jason,

who hadn't said a word thus far, asked, "Do you *always* get up grumpy like that in the morning?"

Coop reckoned he could always count on Jason to restore his good humor. He grinned delightedly at the boy's solemn tone. "Only when I haven't had my coffee," he replied.

They had put on their coats against the bite in the wind, and the mountains seemed almost close enough to touch — awesome, majestic, and more than a little frightening. They rode at an even pace, not to tire the horses; though Charity and the colt continued to frisk and dance across the trail. The river was still nearby, its width a dazzling sheen under the light blue sky.

Toward noon they stopped to rest. Coop perched on a rock and entertained the kids by performing a few tricks. They were more like party entertainments, so Holly tolerated them. A stick appeared magically, seeming to be drawn, by Coop, from his right ear; then it disappeared, as mysteriously, into his mouth. Simple sleight-of-hand, but Jason was enchanted by it.

Then they were back on the trail with the sun climbing in the sky, telling them that time was wasting. After a little while longer, Holly and Coop both dismounted, leaving Jason to ride. The mounts had done a lot of wearying climbing already, and there was more to come — much more.

This, decided Coop, was a good time to get back into Holly's favor. He snatched some wildflowers from the side of the trail, caught up with the girl, and handed them to her with the most charming smile he could muster. Holly was disarmed. She smelled the flowers and treated Coop to something that might almost have been a smile.

"You never did tell me your name," Coop observed.

"Smith. Jason and Holly Smith."

"Good common name," he returned.

If Holly was offended, she didn't show it. She kept her voice level when she replied, "We're special people, Mr. Coop," adding, "Some other people with lesser names might choose ours as a step in the right direction."

"You don't say?" he grinned.

"You should think about it," replied Holly drily.

Coop thought, as Holly continued to smell the flowers and give an occasional tug on the rein to encourage her horse along the stony path. He seemed to consider the matter deeply. Then he tried it out for size.

"Zachariah Smith?" he mused. He shook his head firmly. No, he *liked* his name; it was distinctive, and a number of people were likely to remember it — people who were poorer in one way for having met him but, Coop liked to think, richer in experience. "Zachariah *Coop*," he said assertively.

"Smith," said Jason, who was beginning to enjoy the game.

"Nope," came the reply. "It's gotta be Coop." He raised his voice and flung his name out toward the mountains. "Zachariah *Coop!*"

Coop Coop Coop Coop, came back the echo; and again he bellowed "*Coop!*" his shouting and the echoes spreading and mingling like the backwash of waves at the seashore.

Near the edge of a steep cliff some way up the trail, an ear was cocked to the unaccustomed noise of Coop's yelling. As the sound faded, muscles grew tense, waiting. A round, alert face turned to the direction of the shouting; yellow eyes stared unblinkingly down the trail. Utter stillness; then the mountain lion's tail swished in anger and anticipation. Her low snarl became a full-blooded screech, and her mate stirred and came to her side.

Only the keenest eye could have picked them out; their dun-colored coats blended perfectly with the rock. They were among the great hunters — patient, able to move with amazing stealth or, when the moment was right, with such speed that they seemed to blur as they closed in on their prey.

They were feared, and rightly so. Not as powerful as the grizzly, and not as unpredictable, but when cornered, they would fight with terrifying ferocity. Hunting in pairs, they would run down their prey with a precise and ruthless instinct for the kill. Unlike man, of course, they hunted not for the pleasure of killing, but only when they were hungry. These two were very hungry. Sinews taut, they crouched on the cliff ledge, waiting for some movement to match the sound they had heard.

Coop and the kids came into view some minutes later — all riding now, and looking unconcernedly at the awesome country around them. Charity was nipping playfully at the heels of the colt as it skipped alongside, throwing its back legs up and sideways from time to time in an effort to shake the dog off.

It was the colt that the cats had their eyes fixed upon. The bigger of the two snarled again, and began to slip down the precipitous slope, moving, stopping, moving on again, muscles bunched, belly slung low.

Stealthily, the other followed — two silent, golden shadows, picking their way down the cliff, taking a path that would bring them to a position just behind their prey.

The male lion began to gather speed as the ground became less steep. He was moving smoothly, his great shoulder muscles bunching and flexing, his tawny coat still giving good camouflage. The cats hit level ground together, the scent of the horses strong in their nostrils, and broke into a dead run, swiftly covering the forty or so feet between them and the riders.

By a strange mischance the colt chose just this moment to trot on ahead, leaving Coop, the back marker, blocking the narrow trail. On one side was the cliff, on the other a long drop into a river. The cat had no option but to go for the nearest target.

It was still ten or twelve feet away when Coop and the kids realized something was wrong. They heard the thudding of the lion's paws as it covered the remaining ground, saw the colt begin to panic, and turned to confront the danger. Then everything seemed to happen at once.

Coop had just enough time to be aware of the predator's approach — a streak of snarling, golden power — and to throw his arms up to protect his face, before the cat was on him, launching itself a full eight feet into the air and knocking Coop clean off the horse in a welter of fur and fangs and flashing claws.

"Mr. Coop!"

He was dimly aware of Holly's anguished scream as he rolled and turned and somersaulted down the valley side toward the river, still locked with the snarling cat, trying desperately to hold it off and prevent the razor-sharp fangs and claws from doing too much damage.

The lion fought and thrashed, staying with Coop all the way, until they reached a brush-covered ledge some twenty feet above the river. They went over in an explosion of screams and yells, separating and twisting in the air, then hitting the water at the same time.

Coop surfaced and looked around anxiously. Where, he wondered, was the lion? He hoped the water would slow the cat down; he wasn't looking to tangle with it again.

Then he spotted the neat, round head of the lion some way off, making for the bank. Clearly, mountain lions and cold water didn't mix. The children came as far down the slope as they dared.

"Mr. Coop? *Mr. Coop!*" Holly shouted.

He looked up and tried to signal to the children that they should look to the horses, but it was too late. The mountain lion gained the crest and started after one of the horses. It reared and wheeled and galloped off down the trail. Wearily, Coop dragged himself out of the water. He reflected that he seemed to spend a lot of time getting wet these days.

"Mr. Coop...." Holly looked concerned. "Are you hurt?"

"No, I'm all right." He pulled himself upright.

"Do you think you could make it back up here?" Holly called. He made his way up toward them, accepting a helping hand as he neared the top.

"How's the horse?" he asked.

Holly looked distressed. "It went on down the trail."

"Well." Coop slumped down beside Jason. "See if you can catch it."

"I'll go!" Jason offered.

Holly shook her head. "You stay here, Jason. I'll take the rifle." She mounted the remaining horse and set off in the direction taken by the runaway.

"Did he get you bad?" Jason was clearly worried about Coop, who was bleeding from his right shoulder.

"No," Coop reassured the boy. "I'm just glad that cat doesn't like water."

He sat on a rock while Jason carefully removed his shirt to examine his wounds. He flinched as the cloth peeled back.

"It's just a bunch of deep scratches," Jason remarked, still not knowing quite what to do. Coop dug into his pocket and removed the whiskey flask, which he handed to the boy.

"Okay, put some of that on it and then cover it up," he instructed. "That'll kill anything. Go on," he urged, sensing Jason's reluctance.

As ordered, Jason splashed the liquor on the

damaged shoulder. "Gotta hand it to you," he said as he worked. "You didn't squeal out or nothin' when he jumped you."

"I didn't?" Coop looked pleased, then winced as the whiskey flowed over the raw scratches.

"Nothin'," Jason insisted. "Never saw anyone so calm and collected."

Coop retrieved the flask and took a long pull. *Aha,* he thought, *a hero deserves some reward.* He shrugged back into his shirt and took another long drink. Then he took another. Jason sat watching him tilting the flask, and wondered how much whiskey there was left. Coop wiped his mouth with the back of his hand. "Well," he said to Jason, "there was no sense in panicking." He put the neck of the flask to his lips yet again.

By the time Holly returned, Coop was feeling pretty good. Yes sir, he was feeling *fine.* He scarcely noticed that she had come back without the runaway horse.

"He went right on down the mountain," she reported. "Now what're we gonna do?"

Coop looked at her and waved the flask in an extravagant, careless gesture. "We'll keep right on going," he said, a slight blur in his voice. Then he added pompously, "A good pilgrim does not flee from difficulty."

Holly peered down at him and took the situation in instantly: the flask, the slurred tones, the slightly cross-eyed look. "He doesn't quit them by drinking either," she remarked sternly.

"Medicinal! Purely medicinal!" Coop held the flask up toward her by way of explanation. She looked down at him coldly.

"You have no self-respect, Mr. Coop," she observed.

Jason stood nearby, holding Coop's vest and jacket. He knew what Holly thought of men who took intoxicating liquor. Coop turned to the boy for support. "Did you hear that, Jason?" He waved a hand in Holly's direction. "Her Majesty, the Great Grand Duchess of the High Pyrenees herself has just spoken!" He laughed and took another swig from the flask. Jason failed to react to Coop's jokes this time. He was thinking of the horse they had lost. It was the one carrying their supplies.

"We just lost all our food," he said plaintively.

Holly looked cross. "That wouldn't concern Mr. Coop at this moment," she informed him.

Coop waved the flask around again. "Missy," he asserted, "it has been Mr. Coop who has fed us in the past and it'll be Mr. Coop who will feed us again in the future. Like I said"— he was mouthing his words carefully so that they wouldn't trip him up —"when you're lucky — you're lucky." He rose uncertainly and took the coat and vest that Jason held out to him. "Thank you, lad." Then he turned toward the mountains, motioning for the children to follow him. "Now," he said in slurred tones, "onward and upward."

The children followed as Coop wove an erratic course up the trail. "Stay close," he told them, "we'll have no stragglers." Then he embarked on a clumsy little dance, jigging and turning as the kids plodded along behind.

"The Irish dog dance," he informed them. "Come on, let's go."

Holly got aboard the remaining horse and pulled Jason up behind her. "You should never have let him start drinking," she sighed.

Jason was indignant. "He's too big for me to stop him! Now what're we gonna do?"

"We'll have to keep an eye on him," his sister replied wearily. "The last thing we need is another responsibility!"

The tiny procession had been on the move for some hours when they came into the first snow — large, crisp, unmarked patches of white, taking the sun's dying light and causing the kids to wrinkle their eyes against the glare. The dark areas of uncovered ground were growing smaller as the three travelers progressed; the wind was biting.

Coop staggered on, defiantly. He had stopped only once, to take his blanket and wrap it around his shoulders like a cloak. Then, fueled by the whiskey, he had set off again, staggering it's true, but maintaining a zany good humor. Holly began to wonder just how long it would be before his intake of liquor overcame him. There were no signs of that happening yet, although the flask was still in his hand.

Soon, there was no possibility of taking the dry ground. Their path lay directly over the wide, white patches of snow. *Here we are*, thought Holly apprehensively, *above the snowline. Now it's do or die.*

She looked back, for a moment, toward the valley: its verdant green, the twisting silver snake of the river and the protecting pines. Then she straightened in the saddle and gazed up at the dazzling mountain peak before them. *No good looking back*, she told herself. The trail to Oregon lay over that peak. On the other side lay their inheritance. There must be no thoughts of retreat.

Her horse's hooves made a muffled, crunching sound as Holly walked him on to the snow. The thin, brittle surface crumpled with each step and a minute cloud of frozen dust wafted away in the wind. Up ahead Coop stomped through some deeper stuff, leaving a zig-zag of furrows in his wake. The flask rose to his lips yet again. Then he seemed to realize that they had come into snow. He peered about for a bit as if surprised to find the landscape so changed, but tottered on, grinning, and calling over his shoulders to the kids.

"Watch out for snow-snakes and Eskimo bears!" His path through the snow grew ever more erratic.

"Maybe we should let him ride," Jason suggested.

Holly was scornful. "Better just let him walk it off."

"Well, at least he's going the right way!" Jason, too, had been gazing up at the mountaintop, guessing at the problems that might lie ahead. The wind was stinging his face now, and he pulled his coat tighter about his body, then dragged his hat brim down for added protection. He wasn't too worried about snow-snakes and Eskimo bears...but the mountain looked awfully high and cold.

Coop was beginning to notice that his knees seemed oddly weak. *All this walking*, he deduced, *legs weren't made for it...legs were made to go around a horse...unnatural...definitely*! He turned to wave encouragement at the kids, and the movement almost toppled him over. *It had to happen*, Holly thought.

It really did seem that Coop was traveling four feet sideways — in both directions — for every couple of steps forward. He took a steadying drink from the flask, but that didn't appear to help. The patch of snow he was crossing seemed to be moving — spinning like an ice floe in a whirlpool. *Couldn't be!* he reasoned. He fumbled on for a few more steps. *If the ground isn't spinning,* his fuddled brain told him, *then it must be me! Obviously fatigue, the effort of all this hiking!*

The time had come, he thought, to call a halt. After all, how much could a man be expected to take? No coffee...no food...savage cougars clawing at him and running his horse off...another cold ducking in a river (how was it, he asked himself, that the animals in this country seemed intent on forcing him into cold water?)...then a wearying trek through the foothills, followed by what seemed like a million miles through this Arctic waste....No, enough was enough! He was out of breath and out of strength. He was also about out of whiskey!

He stopped and held out his arms in a signal to the children, letting the blanket fly out behind him, flapping in the wind.

"Hold it! Hold it!" he gasped. "We'll camp here." He stayed like that briefly, arms outstretched. Then, as if pole-axed, he fell forward, face down into the snow, his arms still spread, out cold.

The kids had to smile. Only Charity seemed concerned, running forward and nuzzling at Coop, licking his face, worried about what was wrong with him.

Holly walked the horse up to where Coop lay. "Do you think he'll be all right?" Jason was a little worried now.

"He'll be just fine," Holly laughed, "until he wakes up."

Together they managed to haul Coop from where he lay into a small dip sheltered from the wind and snow. After some searching, they were able to find enough wood to make a small fire. Their food was gone, of course, but they still had some coffee— and there was no problem about finding water. Jason packed snow into the coffee-pot and set it on the flames. Then the children huddled around the fire, wrapped in their blankets, their backs to the wind. Nearby, Coop slept on.

It was dark when he came to. The last few sticks were crackling on the fire. He stirred and tried to raise himself up. It was as if someone had clubbed him on the head. His mouth tasted foul. He made an effort to remember what had happened — where he was and how he'd got there. The task of thinking was too much for him; it simply made the battering-ram inside his skull pound all the more.

Holly was sitting next to him, sipping coffee. He mumbled something to her through thick lips, trying desperately to get her into focus. Words proved an impossible task. Instead, he settled for a more accurate expression of the way he felt. He moaned, like a man about to die.

Holly smiled to herself. *You brought it on yourself, Mr. Coop,* she thought. Even so, she held her cup out to him and Coop took it gratefully. He managed to lift his head in order to get the cup to his dry lips. An explosion of bright lights flashed behind his eyes, but the coffee tasted good — so *good.* He took a couple of large slugs from the cup, then looked around. Jason was sleeping peacefully near the fire, with Charity, as usual, close by.

Holly hadn't spoken a word, but then Coop figured that was all to the good. He recalled her stern looks earlier in the day when he'd started drinking. *Medicinal, purely medicinal.* He winced as he remembered that. He could *really* use something medicinal now!

He took another drink of coffee and handed the cup back to Holly, smiling ruefully at her. "Thanks... good night," he mumbled, and without waiting for a reply — or expecting one — lay down again and went instantly to sleep.

Holly saw his eyes close and watched as his breathing became heavy and regular. Only then did she allow herself to smile. Poor Mr. Coop. There was no doubt he was suffering for his mistake. She was inclined to forgive him in view of the incident with the mountain lion. Jason was right — Coop had acted coolly; and his shoulder had been scratched up something awful!

She'd never have admitted it, of course, but Holly had been badly scared — scared for Coop at the time, and scared later when she'd realized how dangerous this wild country could be. Supposing she and Jason had been on their own when the cat attacked — or that Jason had been its target. She shuddered at the thought, and looked over fondly to where Jason lay sleeping with Charity at his side. She was glad, she realized, really glad that Coop was around to help. It was not an admission that came easily, but Holly was an honest girl: honest with other folk and honest with herself. She was also willing — despite appearances — to give others the benefit of the doubt. But she was fiercely protective of her younger brother. They were orphans, after all, and there were a lot of suspect people in the world; if she didn't look out for the two of them, who would?

Well, she reflected, it seemed that Mr. Coop would — for a time at least. She took one last look at the two of them as they slept, then shrugged down into her own blanket. It was cold and the fire was dying. Holly listened to the soughing of the wind; there were no other night sounds at this altitude. The howl of a coyote or the sudden screech of a night bird would have seemed positively friendly. She pulled the blanket up over her ears, closed her eyes, and within seconds was asleep.

Chapter Five

The blanket seemed oddly heavy. Holly opened her eyes, closed them again instantly against the fierce glare, then opened them once more in horrified amazement.

All around was a vast, thick covering of snow. Jason and Coop were no more than small, white humps, their blankets completely covered. Holly peered down the length of her own body to discover that her blanket, too, was invisible beneath inches of snow. It covered everything. There were no patches now; just an endless snowfield stretching as far as the eye could see. What was worse, more was falling — thick, heavy flakes driven by a whistling wind. The landscape was featureless — blank and frozen.

"Mr. Coop! Mr. Coop!" Holly struggled out from beneath her wet, laden blanket and stumbled toward him.

"What is it?" Jason came awake, sensing, before

his eyes opened properly, the change in temperature and the strangeness of things.

"What is it?" Coop repeated, hearing the alarm in Holly's voice. Then he saw what it was. "Why, it's just snow," he said. In his waking confusion, he'd been ready to ward off another cougar attack.

Jason looked around, wonderingly. "It's all piled up," was all he could think of to say.

Coop took his bearings. Then he realized something was missing. Their remaining mount, and the foal, were nowhere to be seen. He tried to recall what had happened the night before.

"Well," he demanded, "where are the horses?" That had been Jason's responsibility — while Holly was foraging for firewood.

Jason pointed to an empty space. "They were over there."

"Where?" asked Coop.

"Over there." Holly indicated the same deserted area. It bore no trace, not a hoofprint in the snow.

"They're gone now," remarked Coop, stating the obvious. Then he added, "The snow musta spooked 'em."

Whatever the reason for the horses running off, Coop knew that they were in trouble if they continued on up the mountain. On foot, with no provisions, a blizzard blowing up.... He knew, too, how determined the kids were to get to Oregon. He began to weigh their chances — they were not good. Jason noticed Coop's serious expression. A boy with an active imagination, he knew the snow was an immediate worry, but he had some others to match it.

"I heard some wolves last night," he said nervously. He wasn't really sure whether it had been a dream or not.

Coop reassured him. "There's no wolves up this high, Jason." The boy relaxed a little, then realized what had been said. *Up this high.* It was too high, too cold for wolves. And they had to go higher — much higher!

Holly's fears were more immediate. "Now what're we gonna do?"

Coop had already decided. The way back was about as long and treacherous as the way forward. And with the kids' determination to go forward, they'd probably get off the snow faster by taking their chosen route. Either way, it was a big risk. But to go back was to lose; and Coop took only one kind of risk. If you gambled, you gambled to win!

He looked at the kids, knowing it was their gamble too, and that like him, they wanted to win. Well, they'd all freeze to death if they didn't make a start soon. It was time to move on — toward their inheritance in Oregon.

Holly was still gazing at Coop, waiting for an answer. For the first time she was letting someone else make the decisions — and this time she was glad not to have the responsibility.

Coop forced a grin. "Well, we're gonna get off this mountain as fast as we can." He decided it was best to level with the children. "We can't spend another night up here. Wear your blankets."

He bent down and retrieved the blankets from the snow, shaking them, and folding one to go around Jason's shoulders. Then he picked up the rifle — Jason's one piece of foresight had been to remove it from the saddle-holster and keep it by him. With his own blanket drawn tightly around him and the rifle cradled in the crook of his arm, Coop led the way across the wilderness of snow.

They set out as briskly as they could, Charity, hopping from drift to drift and barking excitedly, was the only one who didn't seem daunted by the elements. Coop and the kids kept their heads bowed against the freezing wind and driving snow. Already, their feet were wet through and icy cold. Only Coop looked up from time to time, checking their direction. Otherwise, they kept their eyes down, glumly watching their own feet plowing through the deep, powdery snow.

In all that whiteness, they were the only things moving, tiny and exposed, their progress desperately slow.

As they trudged, the falling snow quickly filled in their tracks, obliterating all signs, leaving nothing but a white, even surface. It was as if no one had passed that way — as if the small band of travelers didn't really exist.

It seemed like hours. No, Holly corrected herself, it seemed like *days*. She had no real idea of how long they'd been walking. She only knew that it was endless. She hadn't been able to feel her feet for some time; but that was almost a relief. The cold seemed to eat into her, chilling her very bones. Automatically, she put one foot before the other, dragging herself on, trying to ignore the pain. Her face felt frozen and tiny particles of ice clogged her eyelashes. Her cheeks were pinched and white, her lips blue; her teeth chattered incessantly.

She prayed to be allowed to stop — just one rest, just *one*, so that she could regain some strength; that was all she needed. With difficulty, she raised her head and looked up the slope to where Coop and Jason walked ahead of her. Coop had been able to give the boy some assistance — steering, half-carrying him at times. But he could only do so much. Side by side, they muscled into the swirling snow, Jason's blanket trailing behind him, his hat wedged firmly on his head. The boy wasn't doing badly. It was Holly that Coop was most concerned for.

It was clear that she was close to total exhaustion. Over the last couple of miles, she had begun to fall back — slowing, it seemed, with every agonized step. Coop knew that if she stopped she was dead. That went for all of them. Their only chance was to keep moving. It couldn't, he reasoned, be much further. They were really high now, well onto the shoulder of the peak, as far as he could judge. Surely they'd be out of the snow soon.

He wasn't convinced. The snow beating into their faces, and the endless, featureless snowfield they were crossing made it almost impossible to find bearings. He could only hope he had led them in the right direction. If he hadn't... well, that scarcely bore thinking about.

Coop himself was tiring quickly. He could feel his strength draining. The cold was like something alive, attacking him, sapping his energy. And if he felt that way, how must the kids feel? He looked down at Jason, battling on at his side, and a surge of pride and admiration ran through him. The boy hadn't complained once, though he must have been suffering. He wondered briefly about the children's parents. Whoever they might have been, they'd produced kids anyone could be proud of.

Holly knew that her steps were shortening, but there was nothing she could do about it. The way seemed to be straight up now; it was like climbing a wall. Her tracks in the frozen snow had become small trenches as her feet dragged. The cold had hold of her, squeezing her in an icy fist. She felt faint and light. Blinding whiteness seemed to be behind her eyes, dazing her. Her legs were like leaden weights that she must drag over this endless, bitterly cold snowscape. The frigid air tore into her lungs, paining her and making her head swim.

Two more faltering steps and then she fell, going first onto her knees, then rocking forward, panting. It felt so good to rest. She was desperately tired. Perhaps just a moment's sleep and she'd have the strength to continue. Just a moment's sleep. . . .

Get up, you fool, she said to herself. *Get up.* It was will power, nothing else, that forced her to her feet. She swayed slightly, gathered the blanket about her, leaned into the wind, and forced herself on.

Coop had seen her go down — he'd been half-expecting it. The kid was out on her feet, he knew. The Lord only knew what had kept her going this long. Despite the fact that she'd gotten to her feet again, she couldn't possibly travel much further. Even as he thought it, she stumbled and fell once more — not going full-length, but simply kneeling in the snow, helpless, drained of all strength.

Coop halted, then started back down the slope

toward the girl. Jason plumped down on to the snow too, registering his sister's plight but too bone-weary to even offer a shout of encouragement. Holly looked up as Coop reached her.

"Holly?"

She lowered her head, sobbing, her face drawn and streaked with tears. Coop sat down before her and, reaching out, lifted her chin. He tried a weak smile. "You all right?" They both knew what the question meant. Gently, Coop wiped her face with his fingers, pushing back some stray wisps of hair from her cheeks. Her shoulders shook with great, racking sobs.

"You're gonna make it," he said softly.

Holly said something unintelligible between her gasps for breath.

Coop continued to speak to her in a low, encouraging tone. "You don't wanna leave all of that land to the stingiest, most undeserving nothing in the world, do you?" She didn't reply, so Coop raised her chin again. "Huh?" he prompted.

She shook her head, then sniffed. "No!" was all she said, but Coop had seen, just for a moment, the light of battle in her eyes.

"No?" he smiled at her. "Well, come on then. Let's go get it!"

Holly nodded mutely and allowed Coop to help her back to her feet, Coop watching her carefully, trying to judge how much longer sheer will power could keep her going.

"Okay!" he said, finally. Together they began to move slowly up to where Jason sat waiting.

Holly glanced up toward the small figure huddled on the skyline and realized how tired her brother must be. "How's Jason doing?" she asked Coop. It was like her, Zach thought, to worry about the boy when she was near dead from exhaustion herself.

"Jason's doing fine!" he assured her. "He's tough. He's like his sister."

Somehow — almost miraculously — they managed to stay upright and keep walking until late afternoon. Coop had carried Jason astride his shoulders for as far as he could, knowing that the boy couldn't be expected to stay on his feet forever. Jason had sat up there with his blanket drawn around his face and his hat brim tugged down, almost managing to doze despite the cold. Eventually, though, Coop had to set him down. The weight on his aching shoulders and legs was more than he could take. Now the boy trudged beside him again, silent, but glancing up at Coop now and then with an unspoken question.

It was a question Coop had been asking himself for some time. There was no end to the snow, no sign of vegetation, nothing to indicate that they might be nearing safety. It was wrong, he thought. There should have been some break in the snowfield by now. He'd brought them the wrong way. Or they'd been doing no more than walking in circles. Time was running out. There could be little more than two hours before nightfall; and he knew he'd been right about one thing — another night on the mountain would be their last.

To make things worse, Holly was beginning to give up the struggle completely. Coop had been able to give her new strength — talking to her that way about Uncle Stingy and the land in Oregon; but Holly's anger at the thought of losing her inheritance couldn't support her indefinitely. There had to come a stage when nothing would force her back on to her feet.

She had fallen behind again and was moving like someone in a daze, staggering, stumbling with almost every step. Her courage had all but given out — sapped by the cold and the sheer difficulty of continuing onward and upward. Each step took a little more out of her. Her brain — her entire body — screamed at her to give up. When she next fell, going down heavily into a drift, she just sat there, staring up the mountain toward Coop, showing no sign of getting up.

"Holly?" Coop yelled to her. "Don't stop, Holly."

He waited, hoping against hope to see her rise. She didn't move — just gasped for breath. Finally, she managed, "Go on! I'll catch up with you later."

Coop knew what that meant. "If you stop now," he shouted, "you're gonna die out here."

Holly lowered her head. She'd had enough. "I don't care," she groaned.

"What?" Coop could guess what she'd said.

Holly looked up through streaming eyes and in a voice filled with anger, desperation, and fear, bellowed it at him: "I don't *care!*"

Coop looked down at the girl as she sat sobbing in the snow. She meant it. He knew she meant it. And he couldn't blame her.

It was ironical, he thought, that if it hadn't been for the kids, he might well have lain down and given up the ghost himself. It was a new feeling, this fondness, this sense of responsibility. Through his weariness, Coop realized with a small shock of surprise that it was a feeling he liked. It wasn't all going to end out here in the snow if he could help it. There was one more chance, one more gamble left to take. He knew that they should have come out of the snowfield by this time. They were over the mountain; or, at least, they'd crossed the shoulder alongside the peak. Unless they really *had* been, walking in circles, they must be close to the edge of the snowline.

They had been trekking up toward the sharp ridge when Holly had fallen. Now they were some sixty feet below it. It was possible that on the other side lay a sight of grass and trees. It should be there! On the other hand, they could top that rise to find nothing but more snow and another hard climb ahead of them. A climb that could well finish them all.

If there was ever a time to play an ace in the hole, thought Coop, this is it. Without making a move toward Holly, Coop flung his arm out toward the ridge above and shouted down to her.

"It's just over the top, Holly."

She looked up to where he was pointing, then shook her head. Good try, she thought wearily. Then she yelled, "You don't know that, Coop."

"I do!" Coop put everything into the bluff. His voice took on a ring of complete confidence. "I'm tellin' you. It's just over this ridge! We've made it! Come on!"

Jason joined in, almost believing Coop because he wanted to. "Come on, Holly!" he shouted, getting to his feet as if to make off.

Holly smiled at her brother's complicity. Well, they were both of them certainly trying. Not knowing quite how she did it, she struggled up on to her knees, then paused indecisively. Coop's voice floated down to her:

"Come on, Holly!" then Jason joined in as they did their best to talk her to her feet.

Now Coop was insisting again. "Come on, Holly. We *made* it, Holly! Come on! Come *on!*"

She didn't believe it for a minute. But she was grateful, despite her exhaustion, to be given a chance to believe. They'd get to the top, there'd be more snow, then she'd give up with a clear conscience. As she rose to her feet she smiled wearily and muttered to herself.

"You're trickin', Coop. You're trickin' like you're always trickin'." But she took a step, then another, then one more.

They watched her slow progress up the slope for a while, until Coop was sure that she was going to at least make it to the top and prove him a liar. Maybe, he thought, he'd be able to keep her going further than that if his guess had been wrong. Still watching her, he reached out and took Jason's hand. Then he turned with the boy and began to walk toward the ridge.

Jason looked up at him. Coop had been so convincing that he wasn't sure what to believe. "Is it really up there?" he asked hopefully.

Coop's tone was level. "I don't know, Jason." But he was praying.

Coop and Jason stood atop the ridge waiting for Holly to catch up to them. They were smiling.

Around them, in the distance, were vast, snow-capped mountains. Below them, leading off from the ridge, was more snow. And beyond that, clearly visible, was a valley with sheltering pines and green, peaceful grass. It was beautiful. More than that, it was impossible! They had made it, just like Coop said. They were across the Divide!

No one spoke for a full minute. Then, without taking her eyes off the trees and the grass and the rocks, Holly asked, "How did you know?"

"It's my profession," Coop replied easily. "I'm a gambler."

And what a gamble, he thought. *Calling Nature's bluff. Crazy! But it had come off. Well, when you're lucky*.... And he started to move down toward the valley, the kids finding renewed strength to follow him.

As they got closer, they broke into a run, spurred on, now, by the welcoming sight of shelter and dry ground. Coop flung out his hands to steady them and, hand in hand, with Charity bowling alongside and barking lustily, they ran until they felt firm ground beneath their feet and the warmer air of the valley on their faces — until they could hear the sound of songbirds and the sighing of wind through the pines.

Chapter Six

They found a spot to camp in a woodland clearing, not far from water and protected by the tall trees. They had all thawed out a good deal by now, but even so a fire was the first priority. Even Charity helped with this, carrying one piece of firewood at a time in her mouth, then trotting off for another.

"Thank you, Charity." Holly put the dog's contribution on the flames, then added some more as Coop dropped an armful of logs beside her. He had also been foraging for food while collecting the wood — just to hold them until he could come back with something more substantial. Slim pickings, but he gave them to the children.

"Wild onions and mushrooms," he announced.

Both Holly and Jason fell on them eagerly.

"I'm starved!" Jason spoke through a mouthful of mushrooms.

Coop joined them for a while, biting into the

sharp green onions with relish. Then he picked up the rifle and got to his feet. "I'm going to see if I can get us some meat, now." He didn't expect to find game plentiful — after all, they were still pretty high. There was a good chance, though, that he'd come across something for the pot if he was patient enough. Now that they were safe, they needed nourishment — the strength to continue the journey. They were still a long way from their destination, and they'd lost valuable time on the mountain. He hefted the gun and levered a bullet into the breech.

"Good luck," Holly said, continuing to eat. Coop smiled at her. "Keep the fire going," he said and moved off into the trees.

He had been tracking for a good half hour without seeing anything, working his way along a small stream and moving from bank to bank in the hope of finding an animal that had come down to the water to drink. He continued upstream, moving silently, looking all the time. There was thick underbrush between the trees, and he was alert for anything that might suddenly break cover as he advanced.

He heard a rustle and stopped dead, looking toward the sound. Just ahead and slightly to the right of him was a rabbit. He raised the gun, trying to find time to take steady aim, but as his finger curled around the trigger, the rabbit sensed danger and bolted. Coop lowered the gun and gave chase.

Having sated his hunger on the raw, wild tubers Coop had found, Jason was trying out some advanced cooking techniques: holding a mushroom on a sharp twig out toward the fire to toast. After their terrible experience on the mountain, the boy was relaxing. Holly had gone off to gather wood for the fire — heeding Coop's instructions — leaving Charity to watch over her brother.

Jason turned the mushroom so that it would toast evenly. He hoped that Coop would come back with some meat. But if he didn't, Jason thought, at least he could give them some toasted mushrooms.

At his side, Charity stirred and growled; then she looked suddenly alert. *Not Holly*, thought Jason, *Charity would never growl for Holly*. Then the dog barked, a series of short, sharp barks. She seemed really alarmed. Jason looked around uneasily. The woods were still and silent. The only sound, apart from Charity's barking, was the low crackling of the fire as the embers slipped. *Holly had better hurry with that wood.*

Charity was on her feet now, hackles raised slightly, her teeth bared, and barking at what looked like deserted woods. Jason peered through the trees again, seeing nothing.

"Easy Charity, there's nothing there."

He tried to quiet the dog by reaching a hand out to her, but she was still backing away slightly, showing her fangs. Worried now, Jason stared at the screen of trees and brush; he listened, too, for some tell-tale sound; but there was nothing to see and nothing to be heard.

Holly had an armful of wood, enough to keep the fire going for some time. She gathered two more big pieces — dead branches, good for tinder — then decided it was time to be getting back. Jason would be okay with Charity, she was sure. Even so, she didn't like leaving him alone out here for too long.

She was straightening up, balancing the logs on top of her pile, when she saw the wolf. It was standing quite still some twenty feet from her and looking at her steadily.

Holly's heart lurched. She didn't move; at that moment she couldn't have moved. Girl and wolf stood facing each other for what seemed an eternity. Then the animal stretched its neck slightly, lowering its head, and yipped three short barks.

Immediately, its call was answered. There was a baying, full-throated and eerie, coming from beyond the nearby trees. Dark shapes slipped through the underbrush, padding silently into the clearing where Holly stood. The lead wolf moved in on her a little, then raised his head and howled.

Now they were all moving, with a terrifying, sinister stealth, closing on Holly, coming in from all sides. She stumbled back a couple of paces, looking wildly around at the circling beasts. Then she dropped the firewood and began to run in a blind panic, back to where she had left Jason alone at the fire.

"Jason!" She screamed her brother's name, desperate to hear an answering yell that would tell her he was all right. Two of the wolves, leading the rest of the pack, were close to her now, though neither one attempted to attack her. They loped along, easily keeping pace with the girl, and edging a little closer all the time.

Anxiously, Holly tried to calculate how far she was from the place where they'd made camp. She was gulping air. An agonizing pain had started up in her side and her legs felt leaden with effort. Even so, she increased her pace, forcing a last, furious strength into her tired limbs. She risked a glance back and saw the wolves effortlessly matching their speed to hers: gray shapes seeming to float over the ground.

"Jason!" She screamed his name again, and this time he heard. Charity had refused to settle down; she had barked furiously from time to time, snarling at the invisible menace in the trees, making

Jason increasingly uneasy. Now he heard Holly's scream and he *knew* there was danger. Whatever was out there had found his sister. He leaped to his feet, with Charity still at his side barking savagely, and tried to ignore the clutch of fear in his stomach.

"Holly!" He wanted to know which direction her voice had come from so that he could face the unknown danger.

"Jason!" She was nearer now; he turned toward the sound as Holly came through the trees, bursting into the tiny clearing where they'd made camp in a frenzied, stumbling run. The wolves were at her heels.

Jason took the whole thing in at one horrified glance. He backed off, yelling, "Mr. Coop!" Their only chance, Jason realized.

His eyes widened in fear. Way back, before they came over the mountain, he had thought he'd heard the baying of wolves and the sound had chilled his blood. The uneasiness he'd felt then was nothing compared to the terror he was experiencing now.

Holly came to his side. *We must stand our ground.* The thought flashed through her mind. *If we both run, they'll bring us down... or turn on Charity.* Then she realized that the dog was much more likely to be the wolves' prey. She remembered having heard that wolves almost never attacked humans. She wasn't sure, though, whether "humans" meant adults; two children would be easier — incapable of putting up much of a fight. And the wolves looked lean and very hungry.

"Keep an eye on Charity," she told Jason. Almost as she spoke, the pitch of Charity's barking grew more frenetic. Her hackles were stiff spikes around her neck and her lips were drawn back, exposing her fangs in a continuous snarl.

The wolves stood silently, as they had before, seeming to calculate their chances. Then they began to prowl, maintaining their threatening semicircle and not taking their eyes off the children for a second. They padded to and fro for a short time before the pack leader paused and gave voice, just as he had in the wood. The others joined him, throwing their heads back and baying in a blood-curdling chorus. Then, as if by some instinct or hidden signal, they began to close in.

Coop wasn't sure whether it was the same rabbit — though he *was* inclined to the notion that brilliant tracking had enabled him to run the animal down. In any case, it was in full view and an easy shot. He brought the rifle up to his shoulder smoothly and, as the rabbit — sensing danger — scurried toward some cover, he got off a telling shot.

The wolves had closed in, tightening the circle.

The children felt as if the wolves' unflickering eyes were burning into them; the deadly fangs were already tearing at their throats. Charity was almost mad with anger and fear now, standing in front of the children — between them and their attackers.

Holly had armed herself with a stick; it was a need for reassurance — something to hold, the idea of a weapon — that had made her snatch it up from the ground. She didn't really believe that hitting at the wolves with a piece of dead branch was going to keep them off once they decided to attack.

"Mr. Coop! Mr. Coop!"

There was desperation in the children's voices as they shouted. Not for a moment did they look away from the wolves.

"Mr. Coop!"

The wolves were close, now, really close; circling, pausing, then circling again and coming nearer all the time. The pack leader trotted forward, checked, then trotted forward once more, bringing the rest of the pack with him. A pause. Then, with a sudden explosion of ferocity, they attacked.

Coop was making his way back to the campsite when he heard the children's cries. He stopped for an instant to listen and heard the flurry of snarls and yelps. It could only mean one thing.

There are no wolves this high, Jason. He remembered his words of reassurance. But they were off the snowline now. He realized that, like him, the pack must have been hunting. Game was scarce here: he'd found that to his cost. The wolves would be hungry; sufficiently hungry, even, to attack humans, but certainly to want to take Charity. Praying that he would be in time, Coop set off toward the camp at a sprint, cranking a shell into the chamber of the rifle as he ran.

The wolves had gone straight for the dog, hitting her and rolling her over in a burst of savage action and high-pitched snarling. Charity was fighting back as best she could, battling against the superior weight of the beasts but pitifully outnumbered.

Perhaps the children could have turned and run. Perhaps that would have been the sensible thing to do — leaving Charity to hold the wolves' attention and fury, while they escaped. It never would have occurred to Holly and Jason to do such a thing, though.

As the wolves darted in on the dog, coming between the children to do so, Jason grabbed up a burning brand from the fire and started to hit out. Holly joined him, swinging a stick like a broadsword, at the gray forms all around her.

"Keep away!" Holly beat one of the animals off, but then turned to find another coming up behind her. Wildly, she lashed out, hitting it, but making it retreat only a couple of feet. Jason was using his burning brand, jabbing it at the animals' faces, trying to keep them off Charity.

They turned and clubbed and turned and clubbed again, but each time the wolves came back. The attack was becoming frenzied now; soon, the children wouldn't be able to hold them off. Whirling and hitting, Holly and Jason seemed to be inside a tight circle of dripping, yellow fangs.

Coop ran down the slope yelling at the top of his voice, firing the rifle and feverishly pumping new bullets into the chamber. He came full tilt toward the scene, shooting deliberately high for fear of hitting the kids. The sound of the gun, together with Coop's wild charge, was enough to make the wolves turn, uncertainly at first, then with real alarm. As the last few shots whistled above their heads, the majority of the pack took off into the wood, leaving two or three still worrying Charity. Holly and Jason smashed furiously at them and they, too, took flight.

The pack reformed near the treeline and Coop sent a couple of shots after them. They moved into the trees like gray shadows — not hurriedly, but knowing they were beaten. The children had already fallen to their knees and Holly was cradling Charity on her lap.

Coop watched the trees at the spot where the wolves had disappeared until he was sure they weren't coming back. Then he went over to join Jason and Holly. Charity lay across Holly's legs, whimpering and trembling uncontrollably.

"Charity? *Charity!*" Holly looked up at Coop, tears starting up in her eyes.

Gently, and with great care, Coop set about examining the dog: feeling for broken bones and looking to see whether the mauling she'd received had resulted in any serious damage. Her coat was bloody here and there, and one ear was torn. Apart from that, she seemed to have come out of the whole thing with surprisingly little injury. Nonetheless, she continued to whimper pathetically.

"She's all right." Coop smiled at the kids. "She's just frightened."

Relief, and sudden horror at what had just happened to them, left Holly in a strange state. Not knowing whether to laugh or cry, she said, simply, "Thank the Lord you came back!"

Jason had found his voice, though. "We were clubbin' them and beatin' on them and everything and they kept comin' back," he said breathlessly.

Coop, too, was feeling shaken. He had arrived

116

just in time — he knew that. Two kids with clubs would've been good for another few minutes against the wolves — no more. He looked first at Jason, then at Holly, and there was a genuine fondness in his eyes.

Thank the Lord you came back! He was glad he'd heard those words, even though they had been prompted by such a fearful event. Then an image flashed across his mind: a picture of Holly, sitting on her horse in a meadow just after the Indians had ridden off, holding a derringer on him and demanding the rifle back. *A derringer!* He turned to Holly in amazement. "Why didn't you use your pistol?"

"It doesn't have any bullets," she stated flatly.

Now it was Coop who didn't know whether to laugh or cry. He gazed at the girl with a mixture of astonishment and new admiration. Then he sighed. "Well," he remarked ruefully, "neither does the rifle, now." Finally, when Charity had stopped whimpering, they ventured a little way among the trees to collect enough firewood for the night.

It was dusk; the fire was burning brightly. The rabbit (which Coop had cast aside as he ran down to disperse the wolves) had been retrieved, cooked, and eaten. Zach watched as the children dozed, happy that they should feel safe enough to sleep while he was there to watch over them. He stayed awake for a long time in the darkness, prodding the fire now and then and setting fresh logs on the flames.

Somewhere, close by, an owl hooted. Jason started awake, looking worried, and Coop placed a hand on his shoulder. "Go back to sleep. It's okay." He eased Jason's head back down, smiling as the boy reached out, instinctively, to clasp his sister's hand. Charity was restless, too; she crept between the children for comfort's sake. Then all three were still again as they drifted comfortably back into sleep. Coop moved a little nearer to the fire and for along time stared out into the darkness.

"Hold it right there, Mister!" shouts Holly Smith (Heather Rattray) to Zach Coop (Robert Logan). Closely pursued by a posse, Coop tries to buy the Smiths' horse. Holly won't sell but she'll let Coop ride double if he'll take them to Oregon.

Just then the posse shows up. Coop speeds away on the Smiths' horse. "Who is he?" Holly asks the posse. "A card trickster who robbed our town," is the answer.

Furious, Holly shakes the rifle. "No one's gonna steal from the Smith family an' get away with it again!" she vows. Holly and Jason (Mark Hall) mount their remaining horse, taking a few provisions from their broken-down wagon.

Coop escapes the posse, but dismounts at a stream and is overtaken by the Smiths. With Holly holding the rifle on Coop, Jason retakes the stolen horse and Holly and Jason ride off. "But you need me," protests Coop.

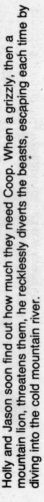

Holly and Jason soon find out how much they need Coop. When a grizzly, then a mountain lion, threatens them, he recklessly diverts the beasts, escaping each time by diving into the cold mountain river.

Later, Coop saves an Indian hunting party from a rogue grizzly. He, Jason, Holly, and Charity, the dog, are honored guests as the Indian village celebrates.

Unknown to them, however, the grizzly lurks outside the camp. That night, the maddened beast attacks and is slain in a terrifying scene.

The greatest test of endurance for Holly, Jason, and Coop was crossing the great divide of the high Rocky Mountains. Here they head into the bitter winter wind, bound for Oregon on the other side.

Chapter Seven

The day had dawned fair and warm and beautiful. Small, puffy clouds billowed above the green slopes of the mountains. The sun was up and the world seemed a friendly place. Slicks of pure sunlight swirled and flashed in the current of the river where Coop was kneeling to shave — performing this task, considerately, downstream of where Jason was fishing. Holly watched her brother's uncertain handling of the line.

A sudden tug told Jason he'd hooked a fish. With a vast, delighted grin, he started to haul it toward the bank.

"Got one!" He looked triumphantly over his shoulder at Holly. "Told you I could catch one!" Coop and Holly grinned as Jason grabbed the fish and removed the hook. Then, despite themselves, their grins broadened as they saw it flip and wriggle and slip out of his hands, back into the shallows.

Jason made a couple of hopeless grabs at his

escaping catch, then stood and watched it swim easily away. "Oh, well...." He decided it was too nice a day to be upset over the loss of a fish.

"That's all right, Jason," Holly said cheerfully. "We've had enough already." For Coop had used his skill with the fishing pole to supply them with an ample breakfast.

Jason was thinking about something else by this time. As usual, his mind was running off at a tangent. "Mr. Coop..." he began thoughtfully. Coop looked up from his shaving. He'd heard that tone before. It signaled one of Jason's questions-out-of-the-blue. Jason looked at Coop sideways and went on, in a casual tone: "... what're you going to do when we reach civilization?"

Coop concentrated on scraping the last of the stubble off his cheeks. "Well, that depends...." If Jason was being devious, he decided, then a vague answer was a pretty good defense.

"On what?" Jason persisted.

"On how my luck's running." Coop squinted at his rippling reflection in the water. "If it runs good, I oughta be havin' a high old time."

"Doing what?"

"First thing, I'm going —"

"There's no need to say it," Holly broke in abruptly, "we have imaginations!"

"I don't," said Jason, wondering what she

128

meant. Coop grinned at him. "Tell you about it some other time," he promised, casting an oblique look at Holly.

Jason wasn't giving up that easily, though. "Did you ever think of settling down?" he wanted to know.

Coop got up and stretched, then squatted down again to clean the razor and rinse his face. *Settle down. So that's where all this is leading,* he thought. There had been a goodly number of people in Coop's past who had tried to make him settle down. *Most of them girls, though,* Coop reflected. It was some novelty for a kid to make the attempt. *Settle down.* That was something Zachariah Coop would never do. He was a drifter by nature; he liked it that way — moving from town to town, taking rest where it was offered, always looking for the next adventure, the next turn of the card.

No, he was not made for sticking to one place... or one person. He wanted to travel easy and live easy and let the chances come as they might — the excitement of riding into a new town with nothing but his wits, and his luck, to provide him with a bed for the night or food in his belly. And if luck didn't come his way that time, if the cards didn't fall for him, then there was always another time. Usually, though, luck was with him. Yes, sir, Zachariah could almost always count on Lady

Luck. *When you're lucky — you're lucky!* A life of risk, of thrills, of uncertainty, sometimes of danger; always a new horizon to be crossed, always a new stretch of country to see — always another poker game to sit in on. Coop loved it. It was what he'd been born for. Settling down was not part of the plan.

He thought all this as he sluiced his face and neck in the cool water. But all he said was, "Oh, I've never been able to cotton to that idea, Jason."

"Can't change the spots on a leopard, Jason," chipped in Holly. She was smiling, though. Coop waved a cheerily dismissive hand at her: "Aaaah...!" and rose to dry his face.

"Let's get outta here! Come on! Move! Move!" Coop had covered the ground between himself and the children in three long strides, whispering fiercely to them and grabbing their arms. Almost violently, he hustled them toward some nearby bushes.

Holly was astounded, then frightened. "What is it?"

"Indians!" Coop all but lifted Jason off his feet and thrust the boy into cover, pushing Holly down beside him a moment later.

Holly protested. "They're supposed to be *friendly* around here!" Remembering their last uneventful meeting with Indians, she couldn't help feeling that Coop was overreacting.

130

"Well," Coop cut her off, "these are wearing warpaint!" Then he motioned them both to silence.

His first view had been of a small party of Indians — eight or so — moving slowly toward them on horseback. Now he could see only one brave, on foot, his face livid with warpaint and a lance gripped in his hand. He was proceeding at a slow, easy lope, weaving from time to time, or pausing to examine the ground. *Tracking*, Coop thought. *Then they can't have seen us yet.*

As if to confirm this, a second brave came into view, walking his pony through some sparse brush and gazing fixedly at the ground.

Coop tapped the children to indicate that they should move out of the path of the approaching braves. Stooping, treading with as much caution as they could, all three moved deeper into cover, traveling some twenty feet before pausing to look around. A third Indian, also on horseback, was circling to the left of them.

"There's another one," Jason muttered hoarsely.

Coop looked over to the mounted brave, then back again as he saw the man on foot coming directly toward them, still searching for signs.

"Get down." Coop's voice was the merest whisper.

They watched and waited, Jason almost frozen with fear, Holly guessing that Charity would give them away any second... and Coop beginning to wonder just what was going on here.

To begin with, he knew Holly was right. The Indians were supposed to be friendly here; and though they were wearing paint, they seemed to be moving with tremendous caution when, in fact, there was no enemy in sight, nor — so far as Coop could imagine — likely to be. What's more, it was difficult to see (though this had been his first impression) how the Indians could be tracking the children and himself. They were coming from the wrong direction — a direction that would have made it impossible for them to happen across any sign of the camp or tracks from his rabbit hunt.

Coop was puzzled. It was still best, though, to stay out of sight. No point in taking risks with a bunch of braves wearing paint. As the Indian on foot came steadily closer, Coop took hold of the children's arms, preparing to find new cover. The Indian came alongside a large, thick bush and dropped to one knee, examining what seemed to be a fresh spoor. Everything seemed terribly quiet. Coop realized, all at once, that there were no birds singing.

Then he heard — everyone heard — the ear-splitting roar. The shock was so great, that it seemed no one moved, no one registered what was really happening. A grizzly bear of enormous size had reared up on the far side of the thick bush where the Indian crouched. Either the braves had found their quarry — or *it* had found *them*.

For a creature of such massive bulk, the grizzly moved with stunning speed. The Indian had just time to draw his knife before the bear was on him: smashing him to the ground and going down after him. The knife was useless, having no more effect than a feather might. The Indian screamed horribly as the great claws mauled at his flesh and the razor-like fangs tore him.

When he thought about it later, Coop realized that it must have been the craziest thing he'd ever done — and he'd done a few things that were *really* crazy in his time. Right now, though, he wasn't thinking at all clearly — just remembering, maybe, what it felt like to be confronted by an angry grizzly.

He could hear the Indian's screams — saw him go down under the terrible, slashing claws of the monster — and then he was up and running, heading directly for the enraged bear, yelling like a madman and brandishing a thick piece of branch that he'd grabbed up as he began to run.

By this time, the Indian lay quite still beneath the grizzly's enraged onslaught. The bear mauled the inert body, ripping and gouging, hurling the brave to and fro in fury. Yelling wasn't going to be enough to distract the beast.

Rising onto his toes, Coop brought his club whistling around in a mighty arc, using every ounce of his strength. The branch thudded into the bear.

Coop swung again and again, smashing frenziedly at the hulking body, shrieking madly as he did so. The bear reared up on its hind legs, turning from the lacerated body beneath him. He was vast. He seemed to blot out the sun. Then he dropped on all fours as Coop started to back off. *He* was the bear's prey now.

As soon as he began to run, Coop knew he wasn't going to make it. The grizzly was too close. There were no trees within easy reach either, but in any case it was unlikely that anything but the strongest redwood could have withstood the strength of this particular bear. Coop kept running, because there was nothing else to do; an instinct for survival kept him moving. But he knew he had no chance.

The children knew it, too. They looked on helplessly as the distance between Coop and the bear grew less and less. It was hopeless.

They had reckoned without the other Indians, though. The attack, and Coop's intervention, had happened very quickly; but the nearest rider had been on the scene fast enough to see what had happened. There was nothing he could do to help the other brave, but there was still time to give Coop some assistance.

Hefting his spear, he rode at a gallop after the bear, reaching it when it was some twelve feet behind the fleeing figure of Coop. Steadying himself, he launched the spear. It was only a glancing blow, ripping into the bear's shoulder before spinning away, but it was enough. The great beast checked, howled in pain, then swerved and ran toward some distant trees.

Coop had heard the drumming hooves and guessed at what was going on. Even so, he continued to run for a while until he was sure the bear was no longer in pursuit. When he stopped, the Indian trotted his horse up to where Coop stood and held out an arm. Coop swung up behind him.

Wordlessly, they watched the grizzly as it retreated through the saplings beyond the river. The children emerged from hiding as the rest of the hunting party reached the place where the dead brave lay. Coop and his rescuer rode back toward them.

Coop stood to one side as the Indians clustered around the fallen man. Opposite him, and further away still, stood the children, still uncertain, still shocked by what had just happened.

Holly, particularly, was still wary. The vivid colors of the Indians' warpaint were fearsome, and she watched the broad, brown features for some sign of what they might do next. Their faces each bore the same stern expression. Indians, Holly recalled, didn't believe in wasteful emotion.

Then she saw the rider who had saved Coop wave a hand in his direction, saying something, as he did so, to the man who was, it seemed, the leader of the hunting party. Coop had caught the leader's name — Mosa — and heard his moment of bravery (or stupidity) being recounted.

Mosa turned to Coop and thanked him in a few brief but heartfelt words. Then, for the first time, he turned to look at the children. As he beckoned them toward him, he smiled.

Holly breathed out in relief. Maybe it was going to be all right. She took Jason firmly by the hand and led him over to join Coop and the Indians.

The grizzly moved aimlessly at first, his brain clouded by pain and fury. From time to time he would rise up on his hind legs, tearing at trees in a blind rage, a furious instinct to kill possessing his enormous frame. His terrible roars and the crashing as he ripped at great branches, splintering them and leaving them hanging, were the only sounds. No other animal in the forest, hearing that awesome noise, would risk being in the grizzly's path.

It was a wild, beautiful country, and its beauty could not be separated from its savagery. Yet, hunter and hunted, predator and prey, were part of an inevitable cycle of death and renewal.

Wolves or cougars would always bring down the slowest or weakest member of a herd, taking out the sickly animals that would weaken the herd. Each species was regulated by another in the wild, from the great carnivores to the insect eaters. Meanwhile the smaller creatures and the herbivores kept nature itself in check, regulating growth, each playing its part in the forest's ecology.

Most animals do not kill for pleasure — only for food. Even when a territory is invaded or a life threatened, a fight between two equally matched animals scarcely ever goes to the death. More often, defeat is accepted and the loser simply retreats. Only man takes more than he needs to survive. Only man disturbs nature's delicate patterns. Only man kills for pleasure. Only man — and the few animals called "rogue."

The grizzly was a rogue. Somewhere in his past, something had happened to make him an indiscriminate killer. The checks and balances that prevented animals from ignoring their natural instincts were lost to him. Even under normal circumstances, none of the other forest creatures would tangle with a grizzly. His power, his size, his fury, made him more than a match for any adversary. But this grizzly was all the more terrifying for his madness — his killing lust.

He had traveled for a mile or so, leaving the scars of his passage on trees, making the forest resound to his blood-chilling roars, before the anger began to fade. Then he began to circle, taking bearings for the first time, concentrating on the source of his anger. Instinct told him that not far away was the clearing where his hated enemy was always to be found — the enemy, perhaps, who had first threatened his hunting ground, who had cleared trees in his territory, who had tempted him with horseflesh and then driven him away when he had tried to take what was his right. The enemy who brought fire and piercing weapons and unaccustomed sounds to the woodland. The invader. Man. Swiftly, and making surprisingly little noise now, the grizzly began to travel toward the Indian village.

Chapter Eight

The hunting party, along with Coop and the children, came toward the village towing a *travois* on which the dead brave lay. The Indians were silent, serious-faced.

Holly, who was riding double with Coop, spoke to him in a low voice. "That warpaint gives me the shivers."

"They're wearing it for the grizzly," Coop reassured her. "He's already killed two people in this village."

Holly remembered the flimsy lance — how it had glanced off the bear's shoulder. "Don't they have guns?" she asked.

Coop shook his head. "No. The White Man don't like 'em to."

They rode in silence for a while. Then Holly said what she'd been wanting to say ever since Coop had run out from their hiding place and straight at the incensed beast in an attempt to save the Indian. "That was a very brave thing that you did." It wasn't, she recollected, Coop's first act of courage since they had met.

He smiled, but didn't show her the smile. "Pretty foolish now that I think about it."

Holly smiled too and dug Coop affectionately in the back. She realized she was actually rather proud of this gambler.

They could see, across the meadow, the tepees of the village. A boy on horseback was leading a loose mount through a nearby stream. Smoke was rising from cooking fires and children ran between the tepees, laughing and playing happily. The village's other inhabitants sat on the ground, weaving, repairing weapons, peacefully going about their daily business.

As the hunting party approached, however, the tranquility broke. A sudden tremor of alarm ran through all, as if everyone had an agonized certainty that something had gone badly wrong. The children grew quiet. Men emerged from their tepees and stood in silence watching the approaching braves. Women paused in their tasks, their eyes fixed on the torn body that lay so still on the *travois*. Then, as the horses and riders came closer, the dead man was recognized.

A wailing went up from the squaws, and one in particular — the dead brave's wife — ran to the *travois* in an agony of grief, her child sobbing heartbrokenly at her side. As the dead man was carried into his tepee his wife followed, wailing still and accompanied by other women of the tribe.

Coop and the children watched all this in silence, sharing the woman's pain and distress. Then they turned to the braves on foot, who confronted them. Standing slightly in front of the rest was one who was obviously the chief. It was to him that Mosa spoke, telling of what happened and of Coop's role in the adventure. The chief spoke first to Mosa, then to Coop, while Holly looked confusedly from one to the other. Finally Coop replied to the chief, motioning with the rifle and nodding agreement to something that had been said.

He swiveled in the saddle to let Holly know what had been going on. "He says we're welcome to spend the night. They're gonna feed us. Get down."

And suddenly Holly's apprehension left her. Maybe it was Mosa's smile. Maybe the warmth in the chief's voice. Or more likely, it was the sight of tiny children in the laps of their mothers, of food being prepared, of men tending the stock or mending implements. Whatever the reason, Holly felt the village was a happy place, a safe place. She nodded comfortingly at Jason and allowed Coop to help her down.

The bear was in sight of the village, pacing angrily to and fro in the fringe of trees and saplings that ringed the encampment. His nostrils were full of the hated scent of man. The thin, piercing smell of smoke, the pungency of cured hides, the aroma of food cooking, the blood-smell of tamed horses.

His ears were full, too, of the horses' nervous neighings, of the crackle of firewood, the dull pounding of pestles, and the puny gruntings of man-speech.

And his eyes watched the figures going between the tepees, the horses shifting uneasily at the tethering line, the children at their games.

The pain from his wounded shoulder reminded him of his hatred as he paced and watched and listened. Inside the bear a boiling, red, unnameable fury was building.

The dance, Holly decided, was a dance for pure joy. A man was dead — but others had returned alive. The grizzly had survived — but courage had been shown that day. Indians grieved, then forgot, as all people should. They praised life and the life-giving wilderness around them, rejecting death and the fear of death.

Along with Coop and Jason, she sat cross-legged on the ground, watching the circling, chanting dancers. There was a solemn beauty about their movements — a dignity — and the rhythms of their song seemed in tune with the rhythms of the untamed country in which they lived. She let the music and the motion of the dance take her over for a time, nodding with the throbbing drums.

She remembered how hungry she was, though, when a squaw approached with a laden plate of food. The plate was offered first to Coop, then to Jason. Holly reached out expectantly, only to find that she was bypassed, the plate going next to the chief, then to Mosa, both of whom sat beside her. Only when the men had taken food did the squaw return to Holly and offer her a share. It was then Holly noticed that all the braves were seated — except those dancing — and that the women were busying themselves by going from group to group with food and drink. Indignantly, she turned to Coop. "Is that how they treat the women around here? They do *all* the work."

Coop smiled. Nothing would change Holly, he realized. She was the most independently minded female he'd ever met. He liked her for it; but it did make her an easy target for teasing.

"That's the way it's meant to be," he told her. "All part of the good Lord's plan."

"I kinda like it," Jason chirped in through a mouthful of food.

Holly rounded on him. "Don't you start now!" Between Coop and the Indians, her brother was learning some bad habits.

Mosa looked at the girl's stern countenance and spoke across her to Coop, smiling. Coop's grin broadened as he replied and a short conversation ensued while Holly's head snapped back and forth as she watched both of them suspiciously. When they'd finished, she turned angrily to Coop.

"What did he say?"

Coop brushed the question aside. "Oh, nothin'."

Holly wasn't going to be satisfied with that. "He was talking about me, wasn't he?" she demanded. "Saying that I should be out there working with those other women." Her voice grew crosser as she became convinced that some sort of insult had been delivered. "Well, you can tell him that I'm nobody's slave!"

Coop allowed a few seconds to elapse before playing his trump card. He watched the dancing in silence. Then he turned to Holly with a look of patient amusement.

"What he said was that you remind him of a strawberry moon" — he paused for effect — "and the yellow flowers when they cover the prairie." Another pause, watching her face. "A time when the buffalo are havin' their young and the world is warm and happy again."

Jason chortled, peering around Coop to see how his sister would respond. She looked scornful.

"You're *full* of it, Coop," she said. But her expression softened. She tried to work out whether Mosa's speech had been long enough to contain so much.

"That's what he said," Coop insisted. "It was a very nice compliment. What's the matter? Can't you take a compliment?"

Holly wavered between disbelief and pleasure. She looked around at Mosa, who smiled at her and nodded, seeming to emphasize his remarks. Holly melted. She turned back to Coop, wreathed in smiles.

"He's a very nice man," she asserted. Then, slightly embarrassed, went back to watching the dance.

Coop winked at Jason. Holly might not have been impressed at being likened to the Czar's daughter, but strawberry moons and yellow flowers on the prairie sounded real pretty.

The day was nearing an end. The faintest tinge of dusk darkened the sky and bird-calls seemed louder in the gathering silence. The beat of the drums and the Indians' song carried through the clear air to where the grizzly roamed the outskirts of the village.

He reared up, a mountainous shape against the sky, and snarled defiance at his enemies, but everyone was too preoccupied with the festivities to hear.

Coop, by this time, had been pulled into the dance, delighting the kids with his clumsy attempts to match the Indians' steps. Two Indian girls, neither more than four years old, pursued their puppy into some trees at the edge of the village, laughing and enjoying the chase.

The grizzly was within twenty feet of them, but he bided his time. His fury was directed at the whole village, the man-scent, the noises and smells that came from the circle of tepees. The girls caught up with their puppy and carried it back toward the encampment, the bear tracking them through the darkening wood.

As they reached the first tepee, a horse whinnied anxiously, followed by another, then another; hooves began to shift and stamp in the grass as the ponies jostled each other uneasily. Then the first hot stench of bear struck their nostrils, panic making them rear and swerve.

Mosa was the first to notice. To begin with he saw nothing but the milling horses, until the gigantic shape of the grizzly rose out of the brush and the ponies turned as one and stampeded toward the dancers.

Mosa yelled a warning, but there was no need. The booming roar of the bear cut through everything, freezing minds for one split-second before pandemonium broke out.

Screaming women and children — Holly and Jason among them — were hustled into the tepees as the fear-maddened ponies raced by with staring eyes and streaming manes. Coop waited just long enough to be sure that the children were safe. Then he joined the braves who were moving toward the place where the bear had come out of the trees.

By the time they reached the spot, there was nothing to be seen or heard. They peered into the gloom, tense, straining their eyes for a darker shadow among the trees, listening for some sound that might betray the grizzly's presence. But there was nothing.

Only one thing was certain: the bear would attack again. The Indians knew it. And they knew that to wait for it to happen was dangerous.

Some time had been spent deciding what to do, and it was fully dark, now: a starless night and useless for tracking. Even so, they knew that the best way to protect the village — to protect the women and children — was to take the fight to the bear. It was sure that he was out there, somewhere in the dark, ready to close in when he sensed the time was right. It could happen at any moment.

A number of big fires had been lit between the

tepees, intended to discourage the bear and give light when he finally made his attack. One by one, the braves lit hand torches from the fires and made off into the night.

Coop joined them, holding his flaming branch aloft and running alongside Mosa. Ahead of him the bright feathers of flame from other torches showed starkly against the black hillside, bobbing and curling as some of the braves began to fan out at the edge of the meadow.

Well, Coop thought, *if he's out there he sure can't miss us.* The idea sent a chill through his body. Hunting a grizzly in daylight is a dangerous enough business; stalking one at night, and advertising your presence by carrying a torch, is plain lunacy. It was the only alternative, though, to sitting in a tepee flinching at shadows and wondering when the attack was to come.

Like the other hunters, he also felt he had something to protect back there in the village. For a second, his mind turned to Holly and Jason. He hoped they were not too scared. Then Mosa tapped his arm as they ran and Coop followed him into the trees.

As it happened, Holly and Jason were good and scared — principally, perhaps, because they *were* sitting in a tepee wondering what was going to happen next. Neither showed fear, of course: no member of the Smith family would, at a time like this. But they did hope that Coop and the braves would get to the grizzly before the grizzly got to the village.

A couple of guards had been posted by the fires; apart from these two, everyone was under cover, Holly and Jason sharing a tepee with a squaw and her baby. The man of the lodge, like all the others, was out in the woods, a torch in one hand and a lance in the other. Holly could feel the tension in her body: the need to stay where she was conflicting with the instinct to flee. Almost trembling, she sat beside her brother and tried to be calm.

The squaw spoke to her, motioning agitatedly with her hands. Holly tried to get the sense of what she was saying, then turned to Jason.

"Must be because of the grizzly. I guess she wants us to stay away from the sides of the tepee."

They moved into the center by the small fire — just as Charity burst in under the side of the tepee. Her one short, sharp bark made them all leap with fear.

"Charity! Where have you been?" Holly's tone carried as much anger as relief. Since the moment when the bear had first run off the horses, Charity had been missing. The dog barked again, then began to cower, whimpering.

The squaw looked anxious, gathering her baby to her and watching the dog's nervous movements. Jason watched them too, remembering how Charity had behaved before the wolf attack. She had been aware of danger long before he had; and she'd been right.

The grizzly moved into the village, skirting the fires, prowling silently. His great head swayed to and fro as he moved. His gigantic shadow, thrown by the flickering firelight, rippled on the thin walls of the tepees.

Charity was rigid now, and quivering in every limb. Her hackles were a stiff ruff around her neck, her lips drawn back in a hideous snarl as she faced in the direction of the bear and barked wildly. Jason and Holly knew. The squaw knew. There could be no doubt. The bear was out there, close by. They moved back behind Charity, staring at the dimly lit wall opposite. It seemed terribly fragile.

They could hear nothing of the grizzly, though they knew it must be close. Apart from Charity's barking and the Indian child's soft crying, there was no sign to indicate that Coop and the braves had failed to stop the murderous beast. But each one of them *felt* the bear's presence, and the pounding of their hearts was loud in their ears. He was out there; death itself circling the tepee, and there was no way of escape. All they could do was sit still and wait.

Then, in one terrible moment of deafening violence, the attack began!

The grizzly's roar filled the tepee, and as the massive head thrust under the buckling wall the children felt as if possessed by the sound. The great mouth was wide open, fangs glistening in the firelight.

Charity dashed forward snarling and snapping at the grizzly's head, dodging the swatting paw that lashed out at her.

"Come back here!" Holly screamed at the dog.

"Mr. Coop!" yelled Jason, crowding back with the others, away from the menace at the other side of the tepee.

The noise had brought one of the remaining braves running. He saw the bear, heard the screams and commotion from inside the tepee, and ran toward the animal, yelling and jabbing at it with his lance.

The grizzly turned, glad to have an enemy within reach at last. He roared again and rose above his attacker; tall as the tepee, and twice the height of the man who lunged at him with the puny blade. The grizzly lumbered forward, swiping at the Indian with all his devastating strength. Inside the tepee, Holly and Jason heard the man scream.

The noise reached the hunting party. As one, they turned and rushed back toward the village. Somehow, the bear had passed them in the darkness; its animal cunning sensed that the easy prey had been left behind.

The flames from the braves' torches streamed as they ran. Each man was thinking of his family, the distant roars and yells giving them new strength, new speed. Coop was thinking of Holly and Jason. He crashed through the wood, not heeding the branches that whipped against his body, his heart pounding against his ribs.

"Mr. Coop!"

It was a cry of despair, now, as Jason heard the bear circling toward the flap of the tepee. Then the flap was torn aside and the grizzly was in, seeming to fill the small space entirely, while the children and the squaw clutching her child screamed and yelled and flattened themselves against the wall farthest from the maddened creature.

With his victims now at his mercy, the bear reared up, roaring in fury and triumph. It seemed to Holly that she was looking straight into the vast maw of the creature, past the terrible fangs that would soon tear at her. It was as if she were looking into the monster's awesome, evil soul; into its black hatred, its unthinking violence — into the very root of its power and lust for blood.

152

She may have passed out for a fraction of a second. Thinking about it afterward, she wasn't sure. But the next she knew, Coop and a few braves were there in the tepee with them, shouting and thrusting their torches at the grizzly's face, making it retreat so that Holly and the rest could gain the door flap and escape.

Holly was dazed. It seemed to take no more than half a second. Coop was waving his flaming brand at the bear and backing out of the tepee with the braves. Mosa was there, too, guarding the entrance with his torch to prevent the animal from following.

It was their one defense: fire! Without hesitating, Mosa set his torch to one wall of the tepee. Others followed suit, running their torches along the dried, stretched hide and watching the flames lick upward. The fire was on all sides, crawling over the walls to begin with, but soon racing all around them. Inside, the bear circled frantically, turning this way and that in a frenzied attempt to find a way through the ring of flames.

There was no way out. The teepe was an inferno. Great bursts of flame shot into the sky. Outside, the children could hear the beast's roars of pain and terror as the fire burned ever more fiercely.

They stepped back from the intense heat, seeing now and then the vast silhouette of the grizzly as it spun and lunged, seeming to twist with the billows of flame. It was a horrifying, awe-inspiring thing to watch. Gradually, the bellows of pain grew less, until there was no sound but the raging fire, and finally, the rumbling crash as the blazing remnants of the tepee collapsed.

Chapter Nine

The sound of the river woke Jason; that and the early stirrings in the Indian village. He lay there for a moment, remembering where he was... and the events of the night before.

He could hear sleepy voices. Somewhere nearby a horse whinnied. After he'd gone to sleep the previous night, someone, it seemed, had been out to round up the ponies. He thought about the bear and shuddered. Then, like the practical boy he was, he put all such memories behind him.

Jason was interested only in what the day would bring — in the future, and in the life waiting for Holly and himself when they reached Fort Williamson and claimed their land. It hadn't occurred to him to wonder how they would manage to work the acreage — two kids, with scant knowledge of farming or the management of livestock — but it was a problem that had weighed heavily on Holly's mind ever since their grandfather had died. She, at least, had some vague ideas about hiring hands; maybe selling a little of the land to get the necessary capital. To Jason, the achievement was all. He'd be happy just to get there.

Right now it was a fine, sunny day, a new day for adventure. He got up and went out into the bright sunshine as the village came alive around him. An Indian boy was standing close by, watching him, and Jason smiled in friendship.

The boy motioned and, looking to where he was pointing, Jason saw two cougar cubs tumbling and playing in the grass. Using sign language, and a few words in his own language, the boy indicated to Jason that the cub's mother had died. Jason nodded, following the cubs' progress as they bounded and ran through the grass, weaving between people, bowling each other over and mewing.

Then the boy tapped his chest and used his two words of English — his own name.

"Red Wing," he announced proudly. Then, with the help of a little more sign language, he asked Jason if he and Holly would like to ride with him. There was no danger now; the grizzly was dead, and for the first time for many weeks it would be possible for the Indian children to roam the lands near their village without fear.

Charity and the cubs romped after the boys as they went to find Holly. They circled the village twice before they came on her and, at first, Jason didn't recognize her at all. She had traded clothes with an Indian girl — both of them standing there, facing one another, a little shy and awkward in their new garb, but equally delighted.

Holly, wearing a fringed, buckskin dress, was showing her new-found friend how to button a skirt. Her blonde braid made a beautiful contrast against the deep brown of the buckskin. For the first time, Jason realized how pretty his sister really was.

He rushed up to her, towing the cubs in his wake. "Holly! Look what we found!" Then he indicated the other boy. "He's raising them 'cause their mother got killed. His name is Red Wing and he's invited us to go riding!"

Holly's initial response was delight at the idea of a ride. Then she remembered their purpose. "We have an appointment to keep, Jason." She was acutely aware of how quickly time was passing.

"Oh, we have plenty of time...." Jason cast about for an excuse to let up on their schedule just this one time. Then he spotted Coop, still apparently dead to the world under a bearskin blanket, and recalled Zach's habit of sleeping as late as he could.

"Look at Mr. Coop," he went on hurriedly. "He won't be awake for hours. Besides" — he decided to play on Holly's innate sense of politeness — "besides, he would say it was bad manners to refuse."

Disturbed by all the noise, Coop thrust his head out. He'd caught just enough of the conversation to understand that there was a chance for a couple more hours' sleep here!

"Go!" he yelled, and retreated beneath the rough fur of his coverlet.

Holly's mount moved under her like a fast-flowing river, covering the lush pasture in great, ranging strides. She never felt so good as when she was riding: the warm wind battering her face, hair streaming behind, the horse bunching and stretching as she let him have free rein.

She galloped the horse at full speed for a while, then slowed a little as Jason and Red Wing came up. They were well beyond the village. Red Wing had been urging them to take a certain direction, and now they saw why. In front of them was a magnificent herd of wild ponies, moving off as the children rode toward them, their backs glistening in the hard light, the drumming of their hooves making the ground vibrate.

As the three riders reached them, the horses

swerved as one, a beautiful fluid motion, and the children turned with them to ride on the fringes of the herd, watching the wind-whipped manes, the stretched, muscular necks and the broad, muscular backs all moving in unison like a rip-tide of bright water.

They seem to flow, thought Holly; and then, like the others, she reined in to watch the herd disappear over the ridge.

By the time they had reached the top of the grassy ridge themselves, they had picked up a traveling companion: a doe that ran along behind the horses ignoring — much to her annoyance — Charity's heel-nipping techniques.

Delighted, the children dismounted, running down the other side of the rise with the doe following in a series of zany, breakneck zig-zags.

Laughing with sheer joy, they ran and ran until their legs would take them no further. Then they flopped into the long grass, fully expecting the doe to take flight once the race had ended. Amazingly, it came to them, allowing them to pet it and eating some scraps of food that Red Wing brought from his pocket.

It was so typical of this strange, wonderful land, thought Holly as she smoothed the animal's coat. One minute all was savagery and danger, the next the country was laying out its wonders and beauties for inspection. There was the freezing wasteland above the snowline offset by the rich fertility down here in the valley; there was the snarling savagery of the cougars to be faced, but they had found kindness in their new friends the Indians; there was the terror and ferocity of the grizzly, and the meekness of this gentle doe. Holly loved it all.

Springing to his feet, Red Wing beckoned, leading them to the bank of the river where it wound between trees: deeper here than where it passed close to the village. They lay full-length, heads and shoulders over the edge of the bank, to watch beavers building a dam. The sleek creatures moved through the water so smoothly; then occasionally they would smack their broad, flat tails on the surface. One such slap sent Charity into the water, swimming gamely toward these new playmates.

On this occasion, though, she had met her match. As she reached the beaver it dived, leaving her momentarily puzzled, then surfaced again on her other side. The dog turned as quickly as she could; but by the time she was facing the spot where the beaver had just appeared, the creature had changed sides yet again, its small, round head poking inquisitively at Charity's flank. So they circled and swam.

Holly felt the warmth of the sun on her back and enjoyed it a moment. Then, squinting at the sun, she made a quick, worried calculation. The sun was approaching noon-time high. Time was wasting. She allowed Jason just a few more precious minutes by the bank, then she called to Charity and gave Jason a look. The boy got to his feet, mournfully. He knew she was right, though. If their land was at all like this, nothing was going to make them give it up — and certainly not the meanest, stingiest nothing in the whole wide world!

All three rode back to the village lost in thought. Jason was wondering whether their land was as rich, as exciting as this, whether the grass was as green, the trees as tall and the water as deep and clear.

Holly's thoughts had more to do with their hosts. She was not a girl to think badly of anyone until they had earned her disapproval. Even so, she had shared the common notion of white settlers then that Indians were savages — given to barbarous practices and lacking the virtues of white Christian folk.

It was an illusion that had been well and truly shattered during the last couple of days. She had seen nothing but kindness in the village — kindness together with an ability to share and work happily together that would have put most white folk to shame. She had witnessed strong family bonds, bravery and protectiveness, and a pure enjoyment that seemed to come from the Indians' ability to live at ease in their chosen land; at one with forest and animals.

Their ways were not wasteful; and although she imagined there could be sternness in their behavior, she didn't believe them to be cruel or vindictive. She hoped that when she and Jason reached their new home they would have neighbors like these.

Peaceful, thought Holly, as they rode slowly into the village. Women were cooking or weaving or tending babies; older children ran laughing from group to group; the cougar cubs romped and tumbled. *Peaceful*.

Mosa passed before them, heading for his tepee, and she called to him: "Hullo, Mosa!" and then, in the same instant, realized that the brave had a face like thunder. Without responding to her greeting he strode angrily to his tepee and flung himself through the flap.

More puzzled than hurt, Holly looked about for whatever it might be that had upset her friend so much. Then she heard the sound of laughter and raised voices — saw the circle of Indians sitting on one side of the encampment with Coop among them — and knew at once what was going on.

Like Mosa's, her face darkened with anger. Gambling! Card-playing! *Tricking!* She was appalled that Coop should stoop to this — cheating the very people who had helped them and shown them such generosity. She nudged her pony over to the group and Coop looked up, grinning widely.

"Hi! How was your ride?" he inquired, then looked down again at his cards.

Holly's voice was glacially cold. "What are you doing?"

Coop chuckled. "Would you believe it? Somebody came up here and taught these boys to play cards!"

With a dexterity born of long practice, he cut the deck one-handed and fanned the cards. Then he dealt, picked up his own hand, and clicked his tongue wryly.

Holly was incensed. "Have you no shame," she demanded, "taking advantage of these innocent people?"

Coop didn't react; he was still studying his hand, deciding what chance he stood of winning a little more from the pile of belongings the Indians had brought to wager. Holly leaned down from her pony's back and shouted at him. "It's just robbing and stealing!"

This time Coop paid attention. "Robbing and stealing? What are you talkin' about? We're just playing a friendly little game. Everybody's enjoying themselves." Then he turned to the chief, spoke to him briefly, and showed his cards, finding that he was holding a low pair against a flush.

"See that?" he asked Holly triumphantly. "The chief just won the last hand. I mean, this guy's tough!" He handed the Indian his winnings, saying, "Very good, chief. Okay," but more for Holly's benefit than the chief's.

Holly watched for a moment, her vision blurred by tears of rage. Then she kicked her pony on, motioning Jason to follow, and made for the tepee where they had stowed their few belongings.

Oh, no, thought Jason, *here we are, back at where we started from.* Out loud, he said, "What are you getting so upset about?"

"I'm not upset, I'm ashamed." Holly had on her face that look of angry determination that Jason knew so well. "Ashamed at being part of tricking and robbing."

"Coop doesn't see it like that. To him it's only a game!"

"A game that only he wins!" retorted Holly. "But sooner or later they're gonna find him out. Then they'll probably skin him alive. And maybe us, too!"

"They don't do things like that!" exclaimed Jason indignantly.

"Well, whatever they do, he'll deserve it. By that time, I only hope we'll be in Oregon."

As Jason looked on, she spread a blanket on the ground, folded it, and began to roll it up with an energy bred of anger. Her wrists snapped the cloth into tighter and tighter folds. Her brother regarded her sadly; he guessed that she was pretending the blanket was Coop's neck!

Back at the card game, things were warming up. Coop wasn't cheating, of course, though if called on to do so he could manipulate the cards with the best of them. No — today, as usual, luck was with him. Not that there was a lot to be won, from Coop's point of view.

The blankets, bunches of eagle feathers, moccasins, and beads the Indians had brought with them were so much junk to him. It might have occurred to him, had he stopped to think, that to the Indians they meant a great deal more.

Coop was holding a good hand and betting heavily. One by one, the Indians folded their cards, none wanting to lose more than he already had. Only one stayed in the pot.

"It's between you and me," Coop translated for the Indian, then added, "What've you got? Show me." The brave put down two pair to Coop's three jacks. Then he rose, disgustedly, and hurried away, almost bowling Holly and Jason over as they approached. Coop shook his head. "It's not your day, Gray Fox," he called to the departing brave. Then he scooped up the cards, preparing to deal again. Holly confronted him.

"Will you please tell the chief that we're leaving now — and that we thank him for his kindness." She added, "We traded the rifle for a canoe."

"Do you know how to handle one?" Coop asked as he dealt a new hand.

"Will you just tell him what we said, please?"

Coop paused in his dealing long enough to pass on the message. The chief looked up at the children, smiled, spoke at some length, then went back to studying the cards he'd been given so far. Coop dealt the rest of the hand, then looked up at Holly.

"He says you're welcome." He spread his cards and uttered a little sigh of delight.

Holly walked off, angrily, leaving Jason where he stood. The boy tried several times before he could manage to speak. Then, falteringly, he managed: "Good-bye, Mr. Coop. Thank you for everything."

Coop heard the pain in the voice. It tugged at him. But he figured there was a principle at stake here. He was enjoying himself. He hadn't played cards for what seemed like years. Why should he be bullied into leaving by a couple of kids when his luck was running? The paltry winnings scarcely concerned him. It was the fact that he *was* winning that mattered to Coop. He was obsessed by the next hand, the *next* fall of the cards. Would his luck hold? Or if it changed, would Lady Luck smile on him again after a while? He had to know! Like all true gamblers, Coop was less interested in winning than in the risk involved. And how could he explain that to a mere boy?

Instead, he regarded Jason seriously for a while finally saying no more than: "You take real good care of yourself, boy."

But he continued to watch as Jason made his way through the village to where Holly, with the help of Mosa and some other braves, was putting a canoe into a shallow part of the river.

Mosa helped Holly to put the blanket rolls in the flimsy craft, then gave her his hand as she stepped in herself. Jason followed, with Mosa holding the canoe against the current. Then Holly took up the paddle.

Coop watched, and to his surprise, he actually found the cards trembling in his fingers. *Crazy! Crazy to be so attached to two children! Crazy to feel so stricken at seeing them go — at the thought of what dangers they might have to face before they got to that plot of land.*

Then another thought: *Why is it so crazy? I do*

feel it. I am worried for them. It's true! I don't want them to go on without me! And without bothering to debate with himself further, Coop did the one thing Holly had persistently accused him of. He cheated.

Dealing quickly, he gave himself the worst hand imaginable: a poker player's nightmare. Just as quickly, he bet everything he'd won on it. The chief's face split in an amazed grin as he raked in the pot; but Coop was paying scant attention. Before the delighted chief could begin to count his winnings, Coop was heading for the river. He reached the bank just in time to see the canoe, Holly, Jason, Charity, and all their belongings turn turtle in midstream!

The Indians leaped into the water to pull the kids out, one of them grabbing the canoe to prevent it from being swept away. Coop smiled and shook his head. *That proves it...they can't do without me.* The thought pleased him. He gained the bank and waded in to help Holly, who had shaken off all assistance and was standing still in the shallows, her head lowered.

"I thought you said you could handle it!" Jason flung the remark over his shoulder as he scrambled up on to dry land.

Coop held out a hand and Holly took it, looking at him bleakly but allowing him to assist her toward the river's edge. As they got there, a squaw came forward and wrapped a blanket around Holly. Still glum, still unspeaking, she sat down heavily on the bank and stared straight ahead.

"You know, you're right" — Coop watched her anxiously, but his tone was light — "I never shoulda gambled with those Indians. They just won back everything I had."

Holly began to cry. Her shoulders heaved and she bent forward slightly as if to hold her misery to her. Coop's behavior had been too much. She wasn't a girl who formed friendships lightly — but when she did, they mattered a lot. She had counted Coop a friend, knowing that he was weak but then coming to believe, finally, that the good in him outweighed the bad.

Now she felt let down. He'd been willing to abandon them both, it seemed, in favor of a deck of cards. The disappointment ate into her. After the hardships, the reversals, and the victories they'd shared — after all they'd been through to get this far — after the initial mistrust and misunderstandings had changed to real affection...

His disloyalty pained her and despite her toughness, her refusal to give up no matter what hardships the wilderness had brought, this betrayal had provoked the tears that she'd vowed she would never shed.

"I feel sorry for you." She looked at Coop with streaming eyes.

"Really?" It was a lame reply. Coop had expected one of Holly's tirades, but not this desperate misery.

"You're addicted to it," she went on. "It's in your blood . . . like an egg-suckin' dog."

"Well, it's a problem I grant you; but I'm workin' on it. It ain't easy for a man to overcome years of corruption" — he snapped his fingers — "just like that."

She didn't detect the note of seriousness in his voice when he made this last remark. Her speech came broken by sobs. "Is everything just a joke to you?"

"I'm not joking." This time she did catch the sincerity in what he said and she wasn't sure how to respond. For some reason, the confusion angered her.

"Now look what you made me do," she said crossly. "The thing I hate worse than anything is a crybaby . . . and now I'm makin' a fool of myself in front of the whole world!" She sniffed and wiped a palm across her cheeks, trying to stem the flow of tears.

Coop shook his head. "No, you're not. Everybody around here has cried at some time or another."

"Not you," she accused bitterly.

Does she really think that? Coop wondered. *Can she really believe that I'm too hard-hearted, too callous, to cry?*

His mind, too, went back to all he and the children had gone through together: the harsh words, the laughter, their uncertain beginning, the moments when they had depended on one another ...on him. He remembered their courage and endurance, the times of danger and the peaceful nights by a campfire when he had listened to the children making plans for the future.

Have I really hurt her that much? The fact that he had the power to do so overwhelmed him. When he turned to speak to Holly again, she saw that his eyes, like hers, were filled with tears. She looked away.

"I sure have," he said softly. "I've cried at everything from bed-wetting to having somebody I really loved die on me...." His voice trailed off. Leaning over, he put a hand under the girl's chin and turned her face toward him.

"Look at me." His voice was gentle. "You're gonna make it. And you're gonna make it on time. Jason and I are gonna see to it." He forced a smile. "In fact I'm gonna give up gambling until I get you there...and that's a promise."

Holly sniffed. "I don't believe it."

"I'll be willin' to betcha..." he began in mock indignation.

A smile began on Holly's face, matching the one on Coop's. Then it spread as Coop began to chuckle. He leaned over to hug her and they laughed together; laughed at the foolishness that had nearly lost them their friendship.

Coop released the girl and called out to Jason. "You ready to go, boy?" Then he jumped down and splashed through the water to where Mosa was holding the canoe.

Chapter Ten

It seemed that the entire village had gathered on the riverbank to watch them go. Jason and Holly sat securely in the front of the canoe as Coop used the paddle to ease them out into the current.

Hands waved; voices were raised to wish them an easy journey. The children waved back, their emotions a mixture of sadness, gratitude, and an eagerness to be off. Time was agonizingly short now. Their land beckoned to them, but seemed to retreat with every passing second.

Red Wing, astride the pony that Holly had ridden earlier in the day, kept pace with the canoe as it moved downstream. Jason waved with renewed vigor, anxious to catch the boy's eye.

His friendship with Red Wing had lasted less than a day, but in that short time they had become real comrades. With his parents and his grandpa gone — and with Holly sometimes having to act the role of all three — there were times when

173

Jason felt hungry for companionship, almost as if he were an only child. If only he had a brother like Red Wing.... But he knew, at least, that he would always have a *friend* called Red Wing.

Even when they had passed out of earshot, the children continued to wave. Then the canoe started to move around a wide bend in the river and the village was gradually lost to sight. Coop paddled smoothly, using long, powerful strokes of the blade on alternate sides of the craft in order to keep its nose steady.

The day was tranquil. Patches of early-afternoon sunlight fluttered like tiny, skipping flames on the river; a cougar, basking in the warmth, watched their progress from atop a sheer cliff — too high, and too far away, and altogether too lazy to cause them any trouble.

They traveled for some miles in near silence, riding the swift current and enjoying the magnificent scenery around them: sometimes high, barren, majestic cliffs, sometimes thick pinewoods sweeping down to the water's edge. Occasionally they caught sight of an animal coming down to drink and once Holly nudged Jason and pointed up to where an eagle soared and circled against the brilliant blue sky.

Their enjoyment of it all, though, was tinged with anxiety. There was so little time left. Holly wished the river would carry them even faster.

The idea had no sooner come and gone, than she felt a tug, as if an invisible hand had reached out and given the canoe a sudden shove. Coop felt it too and held the broad blade of the paddle upright in the water to check the motion. The canoe swerved a little, then came back on course, traveling smoothly again, but unmistakably faster.

Another tug, another swerve: more violent this time, making the canoe rock slightly. Water began to hiss along the sides of the craft and little arcs of spray flew up from the curved prow, wetting the children's faces. Suddenly, Coop found himself using the paddle not to propel the canoe, but simply to steer it.

As they neared a bend in the river he began to look about for a landing place, guessing what these sudden changes meant. It was too late, though, to think of making for the shore. The canoe was picking up speed rapidly, rocking and bouncing. Then they rounded the bend and came into the white water. The children's eyes widened as they saw, from bank to bank, a boiling mass of white and green, foaming and churning over the black rocks at breakneck speed. The water seemed to fold and twist between jagged points of stone, rushing furiously onward yet apparently staying still — millions of tons of moving water that roared endlessly onward.

Coop took a deep breath. Gripping the shaft of

the paddle as firmly as he could, he had just enough time to bellow "Hold on!" before the canoe bucked into the rapids.

At the start, Coop seemed to be in control — guiding the pitching craft between jagged rocks and switching from gully to gully. Walls of spray rose on either side, shot through with prismatic light as they hung in the sunlight, then collapsed over the canoe, soaking everyone. The craft lurched and bounced, coming down on the swelling surface in a series of hard, bone-jarring smacks.

Soon, though, Coop felt the canoe begin to wallow as it rose and fell. Jason and Holly, cringing away from the whipping spray and the rushing water, had moved so far back that they were almost sitting in Coop's lap. If the canoe were balanced, they had a chance. This way they were bound to come to grief.

"Jason! Move forward!" Coop yelled above the roar of the water. But already it was too late. They were floundering.

"We're sinking," Holly yelled.

And as if Coop hadn't been able to work it out for himself, Jason echoed her cry: "We're going down!" Water flooded over the side, filling the canoe in seconds.

"Okay!" Coop tried to make himself heard amid the turmoil. "Just hang on to the canoe! *Hang on to the canoe!*"

That was a lot easier said than done. The canoe was pulled almost from under them by the powerful current, and the next moment they were all in the water, floundering, trying to find a foothold on the slippery rocks. It was fortunate that although the rapids were swift, they were not very deep.

Struggling, falling from time to time as the water buffeted them, all three fought their way to the bank with Coop clutching the children's arms to give support. They emerged from the shallows gasping for breath.

"You all right?" Coop's question was directed at both children. Holly was more angry than frightened. "They told me that river was *safe*," she exclaimed.

Coop knew that to an Indian — with an Indian's river skills — it was. "Well," he said easily, "you kids needed a bath anyway."

"It's no joking matter," Holly reminded him. "One more day — then we lose all our land!"

She didn't know it, but Coop's fears matched her own. His joke had fallen flat even on his own ears. The loss of the canoe was indeed a loss. The river would have taken them toward Fort Williamson faster than any horse — that had been the Indians' advice; although they could still have made it in time on horseback. Now they were left with nothing but their own feet to bring them in on time. Coop wasn't quite sure how many miles separated

them from their goal, but he had a strong feeling
that this last stroke of ill-luck was going to defeat
them.

Looking at Holly, he could see she felt the same
way. He put out a hand and gripped her shoulder.
No one was giving up now — not if Zachariah Coop
had anything to do with it. "Come on," he urged.
"Let's keep going." Together, they began to climb
the steep incline that led away from the river.

Chapter Eleven

They came out of a thin stand of saplings that fringed the hilltop, breathing hard and looking about for the best route to take. Holly was leading, glaring moodily at the ground before her feet and thinking that it was time they had a little *good* luck for a change. All that land, *their* land, their rightful inheritance, going to a miserly...

A sudden rumbling snort cut through her thoughts and her head snapped up. Then she stood stock still in amazement as Coop and Jason came up beside her. Before them, seeming to stretch out over the prairie for miles, was an enormous herd of buffalo, grazing quietly in the peace of the afternoon. They were so close that Holly could hear the soft, ripping sound as a big bull nearest to her tore the sweet grass, his lowered head nodding as he advanced inch by inch over the pasture.

She was astounded. *So many!* she thought. *So many!* The enormous humped backs and brown, shaggy manes filled the eye. This was the Oregon Holly had dreamed of. Awed, she turned to Coop and spoke in a hushed voice. "I told you it was the richest land in the world." Then a second, more practical thought struck her. "Are they dangerous?"

Coop was staring at the buffalo herd in wonder. "No," he said after a while, "we'll just give 'em a *lotta* room." He tapped the girl on the shoulder and beckoned to Jason. "Come on. We'd better get going."

Charity watched the bull as it chewed the cud lazily. These animals didn't seem at all interesting. Big as they were, they would certainly be slow and clumsy to play with. She looked on, as one of them flopped to the ground to roll luxuriously in the grass; then her gaze switched to where a couple of young bulls were halfheartedly butting at one another. Well, that seemed a little better. Perhaps these gigantic creatures could be stirred up after all. It was worth a try. Barking delightedly, she raced toward the herd.

"Charity! Come back here!" Holly's command went unheeded. Yelping excitedly, Charity swerved toward the bull that, a moment before, had been so placidly grazing. With an impudence that took the creature aback for a moment, she began to nip at his heels.

Worried, the children looked to Coop for guidance. He laughed. "She'll be all right — she's just playing. Probably thinks they're cows." He was sure that the dog would be too nimble for the bull — and he was right. Together with the children, he watched as Charity darted back and forth, barking gleefully and easily avoiding the buffalo's clumsy charges.

Knowing that Charity would catch up with them when she'd tired of her game, they began to cross behind the herd, watching the beasts all the time for any sign that might mean danger.

When it came, it wasn't a sign but a sound: rifle shots, on the far side of the herd.

"Hold it!" Coop paused, listening to be sure.

Then came more shots, nearer than before; and to Coop's horror, the agitated herd turned and began to run straight toward the spot where he and the children stood. The buffalo were moving slowly at first. Then came more gunshots, and the herd gathered speed.

As they looked around for some cover, Coop and the children heard the final volley of shots that panicked the animals completely. It was a full-scale stampede now. Nothing would stop them except fatigue. But until that happened, the unreasoning fear that had swept through the herd would keep them running at a murderous speed, trampling anything that happened to be in their path.

"Come on!" Grabbing the children by their hands, Coop raced across the grass, moving so fast that Jason was pulled along, almost trailing behind him. Just close enough — if they were lucky — was a blunt outcrop of rock. If they could get behind that they might be safe!

They made it with only seconds to spare. Flinging themselves into the shelter of the rock wedge, they crouched there with their hands flung over their heads for protection.

On reaching the outcrop the herd divided, still moving at incredible speed. The thunder of hooves was louder and more terrifying than any electric storm. They swept by on both sides of the rock, an endless cataract of muscle and sinew, great heads like battering rams with flecks of foam flying from their lips.

The earth's moving, Jason told himself. *The whole earth's moving!* The tremor seemed to pass right through him. He thrust his fingers into his ears and squeezed his eyes shut, convinced that this terrible avalanche of hooves and horns would go on forever.

Then, quite suddenly, the buffalo were past. The noise dimmed as the herd moved out over the prairie. Dust settled. Coop and the children stood up warily and looked over the rock, almost as if they couldn't believe it was over. Charity emerged from a jackrabbit hole where she'd taken refuge.

That, mused Coop, *was a very close call. Very!* He began to beat some of the dust out of his clothes.

"Club! How many you get?"

Coop, Holly, and Jason all turned at the voice. Coming across the pasture toward them were two men on horseback, each carrying a long rifle, the butt resting on a hip, the barrel pointing skyward.

Buffalo hunters! Coop knew immediately. *Trouble!*

Both men were enormous. The rough, fur jerkins they wore and their bushy beards emphasized their bulk. Rattling along behind was a flatbed wagon driven by a third man. Beside him sat the fattest woman Coop had ever seen.

The man called Club shouted a reply. "Them three over there." He waved his gun over toward the rock where Coop and the kids stood. Three dead buffalo lay nearby looking, in death, like enormous brown boulders.

"Three?" The first hunter's voice was scornful. "They wuz thicker'n flies an' you only got three?"

By this time, Holly had recovered from her fright. It was going to be some time, however, before her anger cooled. She stepped forward. "Are you crazy, Mister? You nearly killed us!"

The riders looked across to where she stood, bristling with fury. Coop stepped up to her side and put a restraining hand on her arm. The one thing they didn't need now was for Holly Smith's famous temper to leave them looking down the barrel of a buffalo rifle.

"Easy," he whispered. "They got guns. Come on...take it easy."

As the hunters rode up to them, Coop assumed what he hoped was a friendly and deferential grin. "Howdy!"

Club sat on his horse and said nothing. He always left his partner, Ben, to do all the talking. Not that either of them cared much for lively conversation.

Ben looked hard at Coop for a while, chewing thoughtfully on a fat wad of tobacco that bulged his cheek. Then he leaned over and spit a stream of rank juice toward the ground, leaving a thick, brown dribble on his chin.

Jason screwed up his nose in disgust. The man's matted beard was already stained brown from the leavings of countless, equally clumsy spits.

"Howdy," Ben managed at last.

Coop tried to speak brightly, keeping his voice even. "Can you tell me how far Fort Williamson is?"

184

Another long pause. Then: "You're lookin' at a good three days' walk."

Holly's heart shrank. "Three days!" she wailed. They'd never make it now. Never!

"Look!" Jason was pointing at the wagon that had drawn up twenty feet or so from where they stood. "It's Lady and Matthew!" The boy was right. Tied to the back of the wagon alongside some spare saddle-horses were the foal and the mare they had lost during the first snow on the mountain.

Coop could see trouble coming. "Whoa..." he warned. It was useless, though; Holly's dander was up! She pointed toward the wagon. "Those are our horses you got there, Mister."

Ben's face darkened. He glanced over at Club, then back to Holly. His words were slow and full of menace. "Young 'un, them is my horses and you stay away from that wagon."

If Holly heard the threat in Ben's tone, she chose to ignore it. "Tell them, Mr. Coop."

Terrific, thought Coop. *She wants me to go up against three giants with long guns and very short tempers.* Still, knowing Holly as he did, he figured that if he didn't tackle them, then there was a good chance that *she* would! He tried the friendly smile again.

"Well, she's stating a fact, Mister...."

Ben's eyes narrowed.

"Uh, we lost 'em up on top of the mountains the other day. They ran off on us." He finished with an uncertain chuckle, hoping that Ben would find the idea funny.

There was an answering laugh, but it came from the wagon. The woman's face folded into great rolls of blubber as she guffawed. Plainly she didn't believe a word of Coop's story.

"Horse feathers!" she chortled.

Ben, Club, and the driver joined in her laughter. Then Ben's expression grew hard again. "Mister," he said to Coop, "I paid hard cash fer them horses an' that sez they *mine!*"

Holly was unimpressed by Ben's mean expression — and even less heedful of his reasoning. "If you bought stolen property," she told him forcefully, "that's your own loss and it has nothing to do with us."

Ben stared at her. She certainly was a sassy one! He waved his arm in the general direction of the wagon, which was just holding up under the woman's weight.

"You want me to have that lady sit on you?" he asked, bringing bellows of laughter from the lady herself and from the other two men. Coop could sense the edge in their mirth. He made an effort to join in.

"Now, the man's got a point," he said, flashing Holly a warning look. "He had no way of knowin' our horses were lost." There was just a chance that they might come out of this with no harm done. Coop continued: "Maybe we could pay you what they cost."

For the first time, Ben looked interested. "Well, how much yuh offerin'?"

"Well, let me see, here." Coop reached into his vest pocket, bringing out some bills and counting them hurriedly. "Forty-three dollars..." Then he dug into a pants pocket "...and eighty-five cents." He held the money out, hopefully.

Ben leaned over and spit a new jet of tobacco juice, less than half of it reaching the ground. "Ain't enough."

"We got ten more," offered Holly.

"All right," Coop proposed. "That's *fifty*-three dollars and eighty-five cents."

"Still ain't enough." This time the juice from the chaw landed dangerously close to Coop's foot. He continued to smile.

"Mister, that's all we got."

"Well, then, I guess you're gonna be walkin', ain'tcha?" Ben replied as he turned his horse's head and started to move toward the wagon. Then, as Coop began to push the money back into his pocket, the hunter reined in. "Uh, that is...unless you'd like to gamble with some o' that money."

Coop fought to keep his voice level; and the kids, to their credit, managed to keep their faces as straight... well, as straight as a poker player's.

"Gamble?" Coop asked — sounding for all the world as if he wasn't at all sure what that meant.

The look of innocence was perfectly judged. Ben was hooked.

He gave Club a look that said, "Easy pickings," then began the business of luring Coop into a game.

"Well, you know, Club here" — he indicated the other hunter, who waggled his buffalo gun in what was supposed to be a friendly gesture — "this here is Club... uh, we got a little game we play out here." He bared brown-stained teeth in something that was intended to pass for a grin. "Sometimes... it kinda helps to pass the time." He let go a positive river of juice. "Called... uh, *poker*."

"Poker." Coop appeared to give the notion some thought.

"Yeah. You ever play it?"

"Uh, I've played it," Coop told him hesitantly. "'Bout once a year at a church social," and he laughed apologetically.

Ben laughed too. "Good." Then he turned toward the wagon. "Fat Mary," he yelled, "get that ol' deck o' cards outta the wagon, would yuh? Me and mah new friend here — we gonna play us a game."

Holly came closer to Coop as he flicked through the dollar bills, recounting them. He gave her a look that said: Gambling is sinful, right? Gambling is wrong. Gambling is for tricksters and villains, a temptation sent straight from the devil, isn't that so? Gambling appeals to a man's lower nature! It was a look filled with delight at the irony of the situation.

In a level voice Holly said, "Skin 'em alive, Coop."

The two hunters, together with Coop and the kids, sat themselves down on a circle of boxes thoughtfully arranged by Fat Mary, who plumped down at Ben's side after draping a blanket over the crate they would use as a card table.

"Are your ready?" Ben drew a pistol from his belt. "The first thing we do is put our weapons on the table."

Coop shrugged. "I ain't got no gun."

Ben grinned up at Club and at the driver of the wagon, who was perched on a nearby rock.

"He ain't got no gun," he repeated slowly. The pistol went back into his belt. "Well, I guess there ain't no reason to put the guns on the table then, is there?"

Next he produced a stained and greasy pack of cards. "This," he announced, "is gonna be five card draw." He emphasized the last three words, to make sure his opponent understood. Coop nodded, so Ben went on: "Okay, you wanna play for the whole thing, or just wanna sorta split it up?"

Zachariah Coop smiled a winning smile. "Well, I guess if we're gonna play — we're gonna play. Let's just shoot it all!"

Ben's smile, unlike Coop's, resembled the grimace of a shark as it closes on its prey. "Good!" He began to shuffle the cards.

"Now, I'm putting up that mare and that foal for what you got there," he reminded them — just to ensure that when Coop lost there would be no confusion over what the stakes had been.

Fat Mary was enjoying looking at Coop almost as much as she was enjoying the thought of her share of fifty-three dollars and eighty-five cents. Her great moonlike face bunched into a grin. "You're kinda cute," she told him.

Coop returned the smile in what he hoped was a winsome way. *Good Lord,* he reflected, *I haven't smiled so much and meant it less for years.* He turned his attention to Ben, who was dealing two hands of cards. "Uh, ain't you supposed to cut for deal?" he asked, in what he hoped was an uncertain manner.

Ben laughed, sourly. "By gosh," he conceded, "that's right. I...forgot." He put the deck down on the table. "Go ahead."

190

Coop cut first, waiting for Ben to do the same before looking at his card.

"That's the A-card!" Coop affected great joy, beaming at the children and looking stupidly pleased. "We won!"

Careful, thought Holly, *you've got 'em believing you so far. Don't overdo it!*

"You won the *deal* is all," grated Ben. "Get on with it."

It took a great deal of skill on Coop's part to shuffle the cards as badly, as amateurishly, as he did: separating them awkwardly into fistfuls and slapping them together into a ragged pile. Ben looked smugly at Club, as Coop licked his thumb and began to deal, banging each card down and frowning as he counted them out.

"One...one; two...two; three..."

Holly was fearful that he'd go too far. *He'll be sticking his tongue out of the corner of his mouth next!* Ben showed no sign of suspicion, though, even when Coop stopped, looked puzzled, and then asked him: "How many cards you got?"

"I got three."

Coop went on counting. "Four...four; five ...five."

They picked up their cards and studied them awhile. Finally Ben said, "Gimme...uh...two."

Fumblingly, Coop handed over the cards. "Two. Okay. I'll take four."

"Four?" Ben's shoulders shook with laughter as he turned to Club. "He takes four!" Club joined in the laughter.

"Four," insisted Coop, taking the cards and putting them with his remaining one.

Ben looked triumphant. "Well, whatcha got?"

"Uh...a pair of tens..." Coop was beginning to enjoy it now.

"Well, I'm sorry, friend" — more laughter from Ben — "but that don't beat two pair."

"...and now I got these three left over." Coop displayed three deuces. "Does that beat you?"

The smile on Ben's face sickened and then died. "Yeah. Yeah, that...uh, that beats me."

"We beatcha! We won!" Coop turned to the children, fixing his face in what he believed might seem a lucky winner's amazed grin. *"We won!"*

To Ben he said, "Now, listen: I wanna thank you, sir; it's been a pleasure. I wanna thank you very much." He got to his feet. But he'd been expecting what came next. The pistol was resting on the table. Ben's finger curled around the trigger.

"Wait just a minute. Hold on there, just a minute." The buffalo hunter lifted the barrel a fraction, then turned his head to spit without taking his eye off Coop. "I'm doublin' or nothin' yuh."

Coop looked around at the men with their rifles cradled in their arms; then he looked at the pistol barrel, angled up at him. He sat down again, desperately playing for time. "Well," he asked, "what're you gonna bet?"

The pistol waved by Coop's shoulder, pointing back to a rangy chestnut tethered to the tailgate of the wagon.

"I'll put up mah papered thoroughbred mare."

"Papered?" Coop came close to scoffing, then thought better of it. Instead he pretended to look thoughtful. "Okay. I'd like to talk to my partners about this first."

He and Holly went into a huddle with Jason, muttering nonsense in order to make it seem they were conferring. Coop put his mouth very close to Holly's ear.

"Are you still carrying that little derringer?"

She nodded.

"Well, then, slip it under me real easy...." Then he raised his voice and addressed the girl in a businesslike way. "Right?"

"Right!" she replied, going along with the pretense.

Coop swiveled back to face the hunters. "Okay, we'll do it. Double or nothin'. Let's go!"

Ben was still holding the gun. "All rightee," he agreed, "but first I want you two young'uns to back off outta here. You're making me nervous."

Holly was sitting next to Coop — as close to him

as she could get. Her hand was masked by his back as she stealthily pushed the derringer under his rear. Then she stood up, motioning her brother to follow.

"Come on, Jason, let's go see *our* horses," she said, glaring at the hunters.

"Go on, boy," urged Coop.

The children walked off toward the wagon and Ben turned his attention back to the game. "Deal 'em up," he ordered.

Coop went through the same clumsy shuffle routine, counting out loud, as before, until they each held five cards.

"Gimme...one." Ben had released the gun in order to hold his cards; it still lay there on the table between them, though. Coop passed the card over it.

"One," he repeated. Then: "Aren't you supposed to give me one back when I give you one?"

Ben looked at him, a faint flicker of suspicion in his eye. "Yeah." He tossed the card down. "You got one back."

"Thank you. I'm gonna take two."

As she reached the wagon, Holly glanced back. Everyone seemed absorbed in the game, even the driver who had clearly taken a vantage point up on the rock so that he could get the drop on Coop quickly if need be.

While Jason continued to keep an eye on the men, Holly rummaged around in the wagon, finding what she was looking for surprisingly quickly. Slowly, she drew the Winchester out from under a pile of skins, propped it against the wagon wheel and stood in front of it.

Ben was wearing a wide smile. He angled his cards toward Fat Mary so that she could see. Without any question, it was a winning hand. Even so, Fat Mary liked to be sure. She palmed the king of diamonds from the little stack of court cards inside her coat, and keeping it below the level of the table held it out toward Ben's lowered, groping hand. That would give him four kings! The money was as good as theirs!

Charity, who had been watching the clutching fingers and the smooth sideways motion of the card, decided that she's like to join in the game. It was a bit like the one she played with Holly, where a scrap of food would be secretly offered under the table. Moving silently beneath Ben's legs, she took the card in her mouth and moved off to examine it more closely. Fat Mary felt it go and smiled at Ben. He simply looked puzzled. Where *was* the darn thing? Not that he needed it, he reflected.

"Well," he demanded of Coop, "whattya got?"

Coop laughed. "What've *you* got?" Even with the gun between them, he couldn't forego the expression he knew he would soon see on Ben's smug face.

"I ain't got much," said Ben modestly. "Just a little ol' full house..." He spread the cards face up on the table. "Kings high."

There was laughter all around the table now, as Coop whistled in astonishment. "Close!" he observed. Then he laid his cards down. "Full house" — he paused for effect — "*aces* high."

The laughter died abruptly. There was silence. Then realization dawned on Ben and he snarled at Coop. "You can't be that lucky, Mister."

"Ain't it somethin'?" Coop battled on with the innocent approach. "I can hardly believe it myself!"

There was another moment's silence. Then the buffalo hunter gave a crooked grin. "Well, I guess it don't matter nohow. You ain't takin' nothin' with yuh. Club," he ordered, "blow a hole in 'im."

Coop was off his seat, the derringer in his hand only an inch from Ben's face, before anyone had a chance to think.

"Nobody move or I blow his head off," he snapped. Club's hand moved just a fraction. Coop jabbed the derringer at Ben's head but spoke to Club. "Get away from that rifle. Get away!"

Up on the rock, the driver was easing his pistol out of its holster. It hadn't fully cleared leather when Holly's bullet caught him in the arm. The man keeled over, howling with pain.

196

"I got 'em covered, Mr. Coop!" She advanced slightly, keeping the rifle aimed. *The Lord be praised*, thought Coop. *She really can shoot.*

He snatched up Ben's pistol and transferred it to his right hand. Then, holding the derringer in his left, he pulled the trigger. The hammer fell on an empty chamber.

"Some people," he informed the ashen-faced Ben, "just shouldn't gamble."

Then he backed off, waving the gun in a wide arc to keep them covered.

"Saddle the horse, Jason," yelled Holly. She kept her weapon steady as Coop ordered, "Okay. Everybody — down on your bellies."

He fired over their heads as they hesitated. "Come on! Get down. You too, lady."

Holly's second shot came closer, ricocheting off the rock where the driver had been squatting. The hunters — and Fat Mary — fell on to their faces and lay prone.

Moving as one, Coop and Holly walked backward to where Jason was holding the mare and the "papered thoroughbred." They mounted, Jason swinging up behind Coop, and then circled to make sure the hunters hadn't moved.

Coop aimed his gun over the heads of the remaining horses and fired a couple of shots to stampede them. Then he yelled, "Let's get outta here!" and digging his heels into his mount's flanks, led off at a gallop, Holly in pursuit, then Charity and the foal doing their best to keep up.

Club was first on his feet. "Some hotshot gambler!" he rounded on Ben furiously. "You let that tin-horn gambler cheat us an' take our horses."

Ben shook with rage. "Now, Club," he said dangerously, "don't you blame this on me. You shoulda blowed a hole in him like I tol' yuh."

"Well, he was pointin' his gun at you, not at me!" Club yelled.

Fat Mary was still lying full length on the ground, squirming and struggling. Getting down there had been something of a problem for her. Getting up was impossible.

"Quit fightin' and help me get up," she hollered. "I can't breathe. Come on, fellahs! I can't *breathe*."

Half mad with anger, Ben tore off his hat and swatted her violently with it.

"Shut up, woman," he screamed. More than anything, he was looking for someone to blame. "It's all your fault. If you'd given me the right card he wouldn't've won."

In his rage, he hopped up and down, slapping wildly at her with the hat as she lay there like a great, beached whale. Then he stomped stiff-legged across the grass toward the wagon, gazing out across the prairie to where Coop, Jason, and

Holly were no more than dots in the distance.

"Dang!" he exclaimed, his face purple, his voice squeaky with rage. "I'm mad enough to eat *skunk!*"

When they were well out of range of the hunters' rifles, Coop reined in, slowing his horse to a walk. They were all laughing, all talking at once. "Coop," declared Jason, "that was the most fun I ever had!"

"Sure was," agreed Holly.

Coop chortled, delighted by his own cleverness. Delighted, too, that Fort Williamson was — with the horses — within easy reach at last.

"Well" — he waved a hand westward — "looks like you'll make it."

Looks like *you'll* make it! Holly thought about that remark for a while. It had been a long and dangerous journey: full of adventure, full of upsets, full of delights. They had found a new land — and part of it would be theirs. But they had also found a new friend: a *true* friend, Holly realized. Land was important. That's what they'd come all this way for. But people were more important than a bunch of rocks and trees and earth. When she spoke, the manner of her words were startling.

"I'd be willing to bet you" — Coop looked up in amazement — "one half of four hundred acres of prime bottom land that you couldn't sit still and work it for a year."

"Farming?" Coop tried to sound outraged, but somehow it didn't work.

"It'd be a whole new future of gambling and high adventure," she continued.

He laughed. *"Gambling* — and high *adventure?"*

"You'd be living with us!"

"Well," he agreed, "there's the high adventure; where's the gambling?"

"You'd be gambling with the elements, with light, cows that kick, sneaky rustlers...."

"You're putting him right off," interrupted Jason. Then he considered a moment, adding, "You're putting *me* off!"

"Those are the odds," Holly stated. She looked at Coop, waiting for a reaction, hoping against hope it would be the one she wanted. The one she *really* wanted.

He seemed to think for a moment. "Odds? We can beat 'em!"

Jason was bouncing in the saddle with excitement. "How?" he asked.

This is it, thought Coop, *I'm really gonna do it! And what's more, I'm doing it because I want to!*

He grinned at them. "If I've told you once," he yelled gleefully, "I've told you a hundred times — when you're lucky..."

"...You're lucky!" chorused Holly and Jason.

Then, in sheer high spirits, they urged their horses into a frantic gallop, tearing across the rich green grass, whooping and shrieking, heading west toward Fort Williamson and a new life.